The Silver Orchid

B.L. Blocher

The Emerald City Press— Southington, CT
ISBN: 978-0-578-70323-7
Library of Congress Control Number: 2020910341
Title: The Silver Orchid
Author: B.L. Blocher
Digital distribution | 2020
Paperback | 2020

This is a work of fiction. The characters, names, incidents, places, and dialogue are products of the author's imagination, and are not to be construed as real.

Thewatchmaker1939@gmail.com

Dedication

I dedicate this story to my son, who for the most part persistently interrupted me by asking me to "Come here I want to show you something." And my teenage daughter who relentlessly complained about working at Dairy Queen. And to my wife who always stood behind me as I was writing this story.

I would also like to thank;

Dante G, Irving B, and Bob O who gave me scores of crazy inspiration. And also Robert H, who always read my manuscripts, and continually encouraged me to make my stories even better.

Chapter 1

If it wasn't for me, either you or someone you know would probably be dead by now.

My name is Dr. Donny Lord, and science is my passion.

I am a Medical Doctor specializing in infectious, contagious, and extremely deadly diseases. I also hold a PhD in Molecular Chemistry and many other specialized science degrees.

I'm the one they call on when no one else can figure out the deadly pathogens.

Don't think that you are remotely more intelligent than me, because you're not. My IQ is basically off the charts: over 205 and climbing. Anyone above 140 would be considered a genius.

What does that tell you about me?

That I'm braggadocious and conceited?

Sure, I know I sound pretty cocky, but I wasn't always this way.

Growing up in Bakersfield, California I was actually a shy "geeky" kid, if they had that term back in the mid-1960's.

I was living in a dysfunctional neighborhood with a bunch of kids who were borderline psychopaths and juvenile delinquents.

I've always been smart, but no one truly recognized my real potential until later on in my early teenage years.

I've always been fascinated with science, ever since I was a young boy.

I think it all began about 25 years ago when my father came home with a chemistry set he had bought at a garage sale. I was only 10 years old at the time.

It was in a large wooden crate which contained all sorts of chemicals, test tubes, hoses and other elaborate lab equipment.

There were dozens of abused manuals and notebooks that someone had been compiling their experiments and logging their data in.

It looked complicated, but my dad just thought that I was smart enough to figure things out, so he let me have it.

In the mid 1960's, safety wasn't much of a concern for parents. No seat belts, no warning labels.

Hell, the most dangerous toy out there was my cousin's Easy Bake Oven. That thing scorched more kids' fingers and started more fires than the volcano at Mt. Vesuvius! The safety regulations for the toys of today didn't exist back then. Probably why this new generation of kids are such a bunch of pansies compared to me and my gang. We survived Hasbro, Mattel and Kenner.

I took that chemistry set down into our basement where I had my own space, and I began rummaging through the box.

It was in pretty poor condition.

Chemical residue was encrusted over the used bottles and some of the chemicals were totally empty or missing.

There was also a kid's chemistry booklet that came along with it, and there were step-by-step instructions of how to make some really cool concoctions such as disappearing ink, and a liquid that could change from red to blue.

My favorite experiment was making a smoke bomb by heating up some ammonium chloride over a flame. And, if you added a little sulfur, it would turn it into a smoky stink bomb!

That chemistry set was so cool! But it didn't take long before I became bored with the lame experiments.

As the months progressed on, I began looking into those other notebooks and manuals that were in the box for something more interesting to concoct.

There were loads of strange formulas and many more other exciting things to create in those notebooks.

I often needed different and unusual chemicals, so my mom was constantly driving me all over town so I could gather the supplies that I needed.

Most of the time the stuff was available at either the hardware store or at the pharmacy. But sometimes things were right in our own pantry.

Things got really exciting when I discovered a formula to make gunpowder!

I initially started out making sparklers on long pieces of wire but soon after I graduated to exploding fireworks.

It was tricky getting the right combination of elements and compounds.

When I figured out that charcoal wasn't charcoal from the grill, but a specially charred wood that I had to make, then my gun powder became really powerful!

It wasn't easy testing it, since my parents were always around, but I would sneak out into the woods behind my house and meet up with my best friend, Marco Delgato. Together we would join forces and we blew up old paint cans, pumpkins and anything else that would make a mess when it was blown up!

Marco was my assistant and the designated fuse lighter. His family moved here from Italy about 12 years ago. He was a year younger than me, but he was built like a rock and looked much older than his age.

His father, Mr. Delgato was a very scary man!

I always thought that his dad was a Mafia hit man because of his ice cold demeanor.

His father rarely spoke to me, and probably considered me too insignificant to waste his breath on. Sometimes he would gaze at me with one piercing eye while the other eye was slightly closed. Probably considering if I was wearing a wire for the feds, I presumed.

Marco was also intense by nature and might just grow up to be like his old man.

If you happened to disagree with him, he would unleash his patented ice cold stare that could intimidate a polar bear.

It was usually unnerving enough for him to get his way, or else it could get violent.

He was the most fearless and toughest kid I had ever known. And, I was glad that he was my friend, but sometimes he could be so arrogant it was difficult to be around him. But for the most part, he cared about me and would do anything for his friends.

By the 4th of July that year, I had most of the kids in the neighborhood lined up at my back door, buying the cherry bombs and exploding rockets that I had fabricated in my basement.

I was making a fortune creating and distributing my homemade fireworks!

Everything was going great until one evening a couple of the North end kids were knocking at my back door.

Kenny Johnson, the neighborhood degenerate bully, and his little snot-nosed brother Ricky dropped by my house for a tag-team swindle.

They claimed to be interested in buying some of my heavy duty fireworks, and wanted to view my assortment of cherry bombs.

But when it came time to hand over the money, Ricky fell short and they quickly left empty handed...so I thought.

I was young and naive.

While Ricky was distracting me, Kenny was filling his pockets with my cherry bombs!

I didn't realize it until after they had left, that most of my precious inventory was gone!

I guess at some point I should have warned them that they had stolen the "lightning-fast burn" fused cherry bombs.

"Oh well, they'll quickly find out for themselves when they light one off," I thought to myself.

Chapter 2

The following morning the tranquility of the neighborhood was shattered as I heard and felt a jarring explosion that came from the north end of the street!

It was so loud, I felt the kitchen table shake as I ate my breakfast!

Minutes later, loud sirens raced toward my neighborhood! I ran to my front porch and saw police cars being chased by an ambulance speeding down my street!

Joey, one of the kids from the north end, was high tailing it the opposite direction on his bike and was passing by my house!

"What's going on!" I shouted.

"Kenny stuffed one of your mega cherry bombs into the valve opening of his father's barbeque propane tank! When he lit the match and touched the fuse, Kabooom!! The cherry bomb immediately detonated, and the propane tank exploded!!

It knocked Kenny backward on his ass so hard, he rolled over backwards about three or four times until he hit a tree!

Ricky ran and told his parents what had happened, and they called an ambulance!

I split because the cops were on their way and I knew they would think I had something to do with it!

Kenny's hand was burnt to a crisp and all his hair turned into ashes!

His clothes were ripped to shreds, and one of his sneakers ended up on the roof of his house! He was having a seizure from the shock wave of the blast and was babbling something about 'Losing his Milk Duds!' I saw the whole freaking thing!" Joey exclaimed as he quickly rode off, riding a wheelie all the way down the street.

Chapter 3

Kenny was in the hospital for over a week. We later found out that Kenny's hand was so far gone that the doctors had to remove a large piece of skin from Kenny's ass, which they grafted onto his burned up hand. It was disgusting! No one ever wanted to touch anything he had held with his ass-skinned hand!

The worst of it was, he had black coarse butt hair growing all over his hand, and it was really gross!

The kids in the school started calling him "Butt-r-fingers," but they usually took a beating for it.

The police detectives were going to come knocking on my door since Kenny mumbled to his father that he had gotten the cherry bombs from me, and his father reported it to the cops.

My parents were sort of going through a Hippie stage, and whenever my father saw "Cops," he freaked out.

I think it may have been primarily due to the marijuana crop dad was secretly growing in the adjacent woods. When he first saw the police in the neighborhood, he actually thought they were looking for him and his marijuana plantation.

He quickly ran out the back door and into the woods!

His crop was easy to find, since there was a path to it from our lawn that developed over time.

Fearing the police were coming for him, he frantically began tearing out his entire crop and poured gasoline on the piles of weed. Then he lit it all on fire to destroy all of the evidence!

About an hour later, when the police finally showed up and knocked on our front door, my father reeked of pot smoke from burning the weed.

The two officers immediately noticed the stench emitting from him, and began to get anxious.

The lead officer curiously tried peeking around him to catch a glimpse of the "Druggie party" that must have been carrying on inside the house.

"Can I help you officers?" he anxiously asked, nervously wiping the sweat from his forehead.

"A teenager in the neighborhood blew his hand to pieces with a cherry bomb this morning. At the hospital he told his father that your son gave it to him," stated the officer.

He attempted to peer around my father and into our house.

My father did his best to block the officer's view despite the fact that there was nothing going on.

He was partially relieved when he realized they were actually looking for me, but then became upset that he had "jumped the gun," so to speak, and destroyed his entire marijuana crop that he had been cultivating for the past several months.

Not to be a stool pigeon, there was no way he would turn over his only son to "The Man," so he conjured up a story that I was away at science camp for the summer and nowhere to be found.

He insisted that Kenny was most likely lying about the fireworks since I was an honor student and Kenny was a dirt bag thug.

"I'm sure he was probably lying to his father so he wouldn't get thrown into Juvie for possession of explosives," exclaimed my father.

"Have you been smoking marijuana sir? You are reeking of it," inquired one of the officers sternly.

"Absolutely not, officer...my wife is frying skunk cabbage for supper tonight...would you like to try some?" inquired my father.

The officers backed away and politely declined.

"No thanks...have a good day sir...sorry to bother you," the officer replied.

The police were satisfied that I had nothing to do with Kenny blowing himself up, and I was relieved when I saw them leave as I peeked from behind the small basement window where I was hiding.

I remained hiding in dark seclusion as I heard my father storm down the steps to the basement where my chemistry lab was set up. He began shouting at me to come out from my hiding spot!

I slowly emerged fearing that my dad was so upset about his pot plants that he might just give me a beating.

That was another common event during the 1960's...beatings.

One day in elementary school I took a survey amongst the kids, whether their parents had spanked them with "The Strap".

Out of the seven kids I questioned, three had gotten the strap, two with the buckle end, and one with a dog chain. One kid's father actually used a bull whip to punish him!

I was totally glad I wasn't that kid!

When my father found me, his face became angrily distorted, and he aggressively pointed his finger at me.

"I wrecked my whole weed crop because of you! Did you really make that thing that blew up Kenny's hand?" he shouted.

"Well...I didn't sell it to him dad, honest," I timidly exclaimed.

I was trying to sidestep responsibility, but my dad was relentless.

"I didn't ask you if you sold it to him. Did you make it?!" he sternly shouted.

I took a deep breath and reluctantly nodded my head, yes.

"I made it with the chemistry set you bought for me from that garage sale.

Kenny and his brother were over, and Kenny stole the cherry bombs from my inventory while Ricky distracted me!" I cried.

"Let me get this straight. You figured out how to make explosives from those tiny bottles of chemicals that were in that chemistry set?" he exclaimed.

"Well, it didn't just start out like that. I started making smoke bombs. Then stink bombs. Then smoky stink bombs. Then gunpowder," I confessed.

"I'm sort of working on Nitroglycerin now...I'm getting close, but it keeps blowing up before I can do anything with it," I quietly admitted.

My father began rubbing his face with his hands the way he always does when he is freaking out.

"All the chemicals you needed were in that kid's chemistry set?!" he asked.

"Well, not all. Some of the things I needed were around the house, like saltpeter and charcoal. But the sulfur was in the chemistry set," I stated.

"Mom has been driving me to different places where I could obtain most of the other chemicals I needed.

There were also those notebooks and manuals that gave me the "How to do it" instructions," I said.

"Let me see those notebooks!" my father ordered.

I removed them from the storage closet and dropped the bundle of notebooks onto my lab table.

My father recklessly scavenged through them until his face lit up as if he had found the Holy Grail.

"Whoever owned this chemistry set before was a drug entrepreneur. Can you make this compound?!" he demanded as he excitedly pointed to a handwritten formula, scribbled on a severely brown stained page in the notebook.

I nervously glanced through the formula and nodded my head.

"I think so, but I need all the elements and materials that are listed there," I replied.

My father then ordered me to put my shoes on, and compose a shopping list of things we would need to complete the recipe from the notebook.

Minutes later, I walked up the stairs from my basement lab and was directed to get into the car.

I slid into the back seat and we quickly drove off to search for the supplies.

"Dad, can I ask you a question about this stuff you want me to make?" I curiously asked.

"Sure Donny, my thirteen year old scientist," he giddily replied.

"What's Lysergic Acid Diethylamide?" I perplexed.

My father just about began salivating in jubilation as he uttered those three letters that would ultimately change our lives forever.

"LSD my boy! LSD...Acid!!" he laughed.

"Isn't that the 'tripping' drug that the hippies are using??!" I nervously replied.

"We are going to make a fortune!" my father maniacally giggled, and I sank down into my seat.

"It's legal, right Dad? I don't want to get into trouble, Dad," I firmly stated.

"It's perfectly legal. Would I do anything illegal?" he replied.

I just had a flashback to his secret marijuana plantation in the woods.

"Oh brother, what am I in for?" I thought as I sunk further down into my seat.

"Okay, kiddo, what's first on the list?" my father inquired.

"Something called Ergot fungus. It says that it grows on rye grain," I reluctantly replied.

I was actually feeling relieved that I wasn't in trouble anymore and my father and I were actually doing something together for a change, even though it wasn't like the most usual father and son activities.

I guess the two of us making a boat in a bottle would have been more the norm, but indisputably not as exciting as making LSD.

"Hmmm, let's head over to that farm supply store, "Bakersfield Feed". We can see if they have any horse oats or cow grain that went bad. Let me do the talking though. Got it?!" My father stated.

"I got it," I sighed and I rolled my eyes.

I slouched in the car seat, drifting off into thought about Kenny's accident.

I guess he could have been killed.

Even though he brought it upon himself, I didn't want him dead for stealing my cherry bombs.

It would have been alright if he got run over by a truck or fell off a cliff.

Rather anything else that I didn't cause would have been totally okay by me.

Chapter 4

My neighborhood was very complicated.

Our street was only a half-mile long, but it was divided into two parts.

The Northies and the Southies.

The North end of the street was inhabited by the degenerate riff-raff kids, "The Northies," as they were commonly referred to.

They were mostly dysfunctional psychopaths who were school skipping, drug addicted, alcoholic, criminal losers. On the South end of my street (where I lived) were the kids who were into sports, clean cut and a bit nerdy.

They were the jocks and honor students.

The wedge was so deep between the two, we seldom crossed paths.

My house was right on the border. I guess you could say that I was at the equator.

Although I had mostly associated with the sporty and nerdy kids, I had fostered some acquaintances north of the border, especially since some of them were my best fireworks customers.

But there was another special reason for my association with the Northies.

Her name was Kelly Mosley.

She was the most beautiful girl on my street, in my town, in my state, and in my entire world, as far as I was concerned.

She had long cocoa brown hair and dark hazel eyes.

She was a bit of a tomboy, and we played together every day when we were kids in elementary school.

Her father used to joke with me, and ask me if I wanted to "fight him" whenever I was over visiting their house, as he puffed smoke from his cigarette, as it always hung on the edge of his lip.

I had known Kelly since we were in the first grade. She was my first and only crush.

We spent so much time together after school and during the summer breaks.

We were together almost every day and she was my best friend in the world.

Those days with Kelly, were the best years of my life.

Chapter 5

One summer morning as I was exploring out in the woods far behind my house, I had found a special place.

A secret cove deep in the woods where there was a running brook and a tall waterfall which emptied into a crystal clear pond.

The water was cold, crisp and clear, and I would sometimes drink it right from the waterfall.

I brought Kelly there one beautiful sunny day.

It was the last day of summer vacation and the day before middle school was to start.

She was amazed by its peaceful serenity, and the beauty of my secret place.

"I wish I could be that waterfall. It's so peaceful at the top, but then it violently crashes into the rocks below, and then becomes peaceful again as the clear water makes its way into the pond," she philosophically stated.

Then without any hesitation she grabbed my arm, and we jumped into the pond!

It was freezing cold, but it was something I never would have done on my own.

She had that bit of a wild side about her, and she brought that out of me too.

When we crawled out of the water, we laid next to each other on the soft grass, at the pond's edge, and let the warm sun bask down on us as we stared up at the sky. We watched the birds flying overhead and the fluffy clouds drift by.

Our fingers touched, and she immediately took hold of my hand, and held it tightly as we called out the unusual cloud shapes that floated by.

Her hand was so soft and warm. I never wanted to let go of her. We stayed there for a while and I wanted to kiss her so badly, but I suppose I was too nervous that maybe she didn't feel the same way about me.

Till the day I die, I'll always cherish that day at the waterfall, because I loved her with all my heart.

Chapter 6

That following day began the start of middle school, and Kelly and I were separated.

Kelly's parents had sent her to a parochial school across town, and I went to the public Jr. high school along with most of the other kids on my street.

Oddly, after that day at the waterfall, I never saw Kelly.

I didn't understand why she became so reclusive.

I would ride my bike by her house every day, hoping that she might just see me, and bolt out of her front door as I was passing by and tackle me off my bike! She could then confess her unbridled love and passion for me and smother me with kisses.

Unfortunately, that never happened.

I never saw her, and I suspected that her father kept her in chains and locked her in her room.

Maybe she found new friends at her new school and I wasn't so important anymore.

I couldn't bring it on myself to just go and knock on her door. I don't know why that would have been so awkward for me, after all she was my best friend. Maybe I was afraid that she wasn't interested in being my friend anymore, this way at least there was still hope for us.

Chapter 7

The car screeched to a halt as we arrived at the feed store.

My father ordered me to wait in the car as he spied out a grungy looking young man in his early twenties, who worked there.

He had long blonde hair down to his shoulders and was wearing a "Make Love not War" tee shirt and faded ripped up bell bottom jeans.

My father approached him, and they were having a discreet conversation.

The young man excitedly nodded his head and briskly disappeared into one of the storage sheds.

About a minute later he returned with a large burlap sack on his shoulder. "RYE SEED" was printed across it in large red letters.

He followed my father to the car, and as my father opened the trunk, and he tossed it in.

I felt the car sink and drop as the bag hit the floor of the trunk and my father slammed it closed.

The two then did a bit of yucking it up and back slapping, and then my father walked back to the car.

"Aren't you going to pay for it?!" I asked.

"The grain was no good...loaded with black ergo fungus!" he laughed as he got in and started the car.

"Well that was easy! That guy knew exactly what we needed. Next stop the pet store. We need to buy some rodents to experiment on," stated my father.

"You mean you are finally going to buy me the Hamster I've been begging for since I was 5 years old?!" I exclaimed.

"Uhh no. I'm going to buy you a bunch of ugly rats, and we are going to see if you can make them want to fly like Lucy in the sky with diamonds," he sarcastically replied.

"Gee thanks," I scoffed.

By the end of the day, we managed to find the balance of the materials needed to produce the LSD.

I was stuck in my basement lab under my dad's oppressive supervision, growing fungus and mixing chemicals into different compounds. Arduously working to fabricate the LSD.

It was just so boring though!

Occasionally I would slip back into my nitroglycerin experiments, just to have some fun when my dad wasn't around.

As the weeks crept on, I diligently tweaked the book's instructions, and at last we had our first test batch of LSD. I dipped a small piece of cheese into the crusty powder and I fed it to the one rat that I disliked most.

His name was "Crud".

He was an ugly brown rat with a scabby stub of a tail.

He was the Kenny Johnson of the rat farm, always bullying all the other rats, and taking their food from them.

After about 20 seconds of the cheese consumption, Crud jumped on his wire wheel and began running wildly out of control! But oddly, only using his hind legs!

It was the strangest thing I had ever seen!

He was plowing his head around that running wheel.

After about a minute of that, he pushed himself off the wheel and hopped up and down on his two hind feet for a few minutes!

He was actually hitting the roof of the cage!!

Finally he did a few backward flips, and then passed out for about an hour before he woke up and showed some movement in his front feet again!

My father sternly watched Crud revive, and began rubbing his hands together. I could see the dollar signs in his eyes!

"Money…lots and lots of money," he salivated.

"Now we need a bigger test subject!" my father exclaimed.

As if on cue, we heard the aggravating barking sound of our next door neighbor's EXTREMELY AGGRESSIVE, jet black pit bull dog named "Chomper", and we both gazed at each other and nodded our heads in agreement.

Chomper was well known by every kid, jogger and mailman in the neighborhood.

He once got loose and killed a ferocious brahma bull that resided at the farm at the end of our street.

He ripped apart that vicious bull's throat and it was dead in less than two minutes!

That dog is one bad son of a bitch!

When the farmer frantically contacted the police, they sent over the animal control officer to bring Chomper in.

When the officer arrived at the farm, Chomper was actually feeding off the bull, tearing pieces of the bulls tongue out of its mouth and gulping it down his throat without chewing it.

The officer was holding a tiny nylon leash when he exited his truck.

Quickly realizing what he was in for, he opted to return to his truck and retrieved something more appropriate. A long thick pole about six feet long, with a rope noose attached to the end of it.

I think the idea was to slip the noose over Chomper's head, and use the stick to keep him away as he pushed him into a cage.

When the officer approached Chomper, he began to viciously growl.

In dog's speech he was saying;

"Stay the hell away from my meat!".

The officer nervously approached Chomper, but before he could lift the pole, Chomper sprung and attacked the officer!

He clamped his massive Jaws onto the officer's elbow and then Chomper twisted his massive body and flipped the man over, sinking his teeth in even deeper and he grotesquely tore off the officer's arm at the elbow joint!

The farmer who was watching from afar, quickly called the police again!

This time they responded by sending out the elite SWAT team.

When the SWAT team finally arrived, they were aiming to shoot Chomper as he was laying on top of that poor unconscious animal control officer, lapping up the blood which was gushing out of his severed arm.

When the SWAT team began shooting, Chomper quickly picked up the man's arm, and scurried off with it into the woods!

He disappeared and they were never able to track him down.

A few weeks had passed when everything had finally settled down.

Chomper then came strolling out of the woods, still gnawing on the skeletal arm remains of that poor animal control officer.

Chomper's owner (Mr. Bundy) hid him in their basement for weeks until the heat died down.

He said he would never let the cops take Chomper to the joint and give him the chair!

Mr. Bundy was also a really atrocious man.

He was actually a "Hells Angel" biker (so he claimed), and he worked as a bouncer at a local biker bar.

He was a big burly man in his 40's with a long unkempt beard and a scar across his nose.

Rumor has it that he was hitting on another biker's girlfriend at the bar one night, and the boyfriend smashed a whiskey bottle across his face!

That's how he got the scar.

Mr. Bundy proceeded to put that guy into the hospital...not for smashing the bottle across his face, but because it was his whisky bottle and it was still half full of good liquor!

He actually wound up marrying that guy's woman!

She was incredibly beautiful, and I often wondered how a bum like Bundy ever got a trophy wife like her.

Why would she be with a big fat, gross, ugly guy like Mr. Bundy?

I don't think it was because of his sparkling personality or because he had money. It had to be more than that. Maybe she is just one of those psychos who is attracted to losers?

During the summer, I would sometimes spy on her from my bedroom window as she sunbathed in their backyard.

I'm sure she knew I was watching her, too.

She would aim her chair directly at me, and occasionally her top would just "accidentally" fall off, and she would smile and glance up at my window!

No one actually knew where Chomper came from, but there was a story floating around that Mr. Bundy found Chomper when he was just a puppy.

He was feeding on a mountain lion carcass on the side of an old dirt road as Mr. Bundy was driving by on his motorcycle.

No one is sure if baby Chomper actually killed that mountain lion or if it was road kill, but it's likely Chomper did kill it.

Mr. Bundy rode toward him, and reached down and scooped him up one handed by the back of his neck, dangling the pup off to the side as he charged down the street on his Harley Davidson motorcycle.

Now Chomper is all grown up, and very large!

His head is as big as a basketball with fierce demonic blue eyes!

He has giant shark-like teeth and massive crocodile jaws! His body was black as coal, smooth and sleek. He probably weighed close to 225 pounds, and is a mortar shell of an extremely, violently aggressive dog!

If your cat is missing, Chomper most likely ate it as a snack.

Mr. Bundy could barely hold Chomper back as they took their "tug of war" walks down our street.

Frequently, Chomper would pull Mr. Bundy down and drag him on his belly across the street or through someone's yard as he chased after something.

However, Mr. Bundy would never let go of that heavy chain leash, and after a short time, Chomper would eventually tire.

Mr. Bundy would then manage the strength to get up and continue his walk.

Everyone would run into their houses or cars and lock their doors whenever they were coming.

If you drove your car too close, Chomper was known to take a bite out of your fender too!

Chapter 8

My father left my basement lab, and went up to the kitchen, returning with a frozen hot dog.

"What are you going to do with that wiener?" I asked.

"We are going to send this wiener over to Chomper with a little flower power sprinkled on it!" he exclaimed.

"How are you going to get close enough to give it to him before he kills you?" I chuckled.

"Easy, we are going to send it via "airmail" over the fence!" he laughed.

My father took the hot dog, and carefully dipped and rolled the end into the crusty LSD powder.

We excitedly rushed all the way back up the stairs up into my bedroom, which overlooked Chompers backyard.

We saw that he was chained to his dog house with a very heavy steel chain and was passing the time by tearing up a doll which he had taken from someone's yard on his morning prowl.

My father looked around to see if anyone was watching, and when he was sure that the coast was clear, he tossed the hot dog out my window, over the fence, and into Chompers domain.

When Chomper heard the "thud" of the hot dog hitting the ground he became curious, and began sniffing around at the torn up grass until he came across the hot dog lying in the dirt.

It landed right next to one of his huge piles of dog crap, but Chomper didn't seem to care.

He instantly began sniffing at it, but refused to pick it up and eat it.

"I think you should have put some mustard on it!" I joked.

Chomper then began pushing it around with his nose, until he finally picked up the hot dog by the opposite end, and he began walking the fence line back and forth while holding that hot dog like a bent cigar in his mouth!

"C'mon you stupid mutt…eat that hot dog!" my father shouted.

Just then we heard their back door open and slam closed as Mr. Bundy came out of the house with his heavy chain leash.

Fearing his hot dog would get eaten by his owner, Chomper quickly gulped it down in two bites!

"I guess we didn't need the mustard after all," I whispered.

Mr. Bundy attached the leash to Chomper's spiked collar and he jerked Mr. Bundy toward the street.

He was ready to begin his hunt.

We stormed down the stairs, and rushed outside hiding behind the old oak tree in our yard.

We peeked down the sidewalk curiously watching Chomper and Mr. Bundy wrestling their way down the street.

Suddenly without notice Chomper slowly began zigzagging across the sidewalk, then he paused and began squirting pee on Mr. Bundy's leg!

His head drooped completely to the ground, and he continued zigzagging incoherently all over the sidewalk with his front legs paralyzed.

His head was just plowing over the concrete and grass. Mr. Bundy started shaking the leash and lifting his head up, but Chomper was obviously "tripping" out!

Mr. Bundy became concerned and desperately tried dragging Chomper back toward his house.

They were passing Mrs. Bugnacki's yard (the neighborhood busybody), which was decorated with a variety of life like concrete wildlife statuaries.

Chomper's front legs suddenly engaged and he began dragging Mr. Bundy into her yard and right for her cute little Bambi deer statuary, and he began humping all over it!

Mr. Bundy panicked, and desperately tried pulling Chomper off Bambi!

But Chomper had turned into a nymphomaniac super dog and kept wildly going at it!

Drool and semen were spraying all over the place, and drenching poor little Bambi!

Mrs. Bugnacki saw what was happening from her kitchen window, and came charging off of her porch hysterically with a broom in hand, screaming her head off!

"Get that horny mutt away from my Bambi you perverts!" she shouted.

My father and I were laughing hysterically as we hid behind our tree!

Just then Chomper pulled the chain free from Mr. Bundy's grip, and ran away chasing his shadow toward our yard, with Mr. Bundy giving chase right behind him!

We scrambled toward our car and jumped in as Chomper was closing in on us.

As my father slammed the heavy car door closed, we cringed as Chomper jumped at our 1957 Chevy Bel Air. He soared through the air for a few seconds, until he finally crashed head first into our windshield!

With his tongue hanging out, and his face pressed against the glass, he slowly slid down the windshield and laid motionless on his back with his feet pointing straight up to the sky!

"Is he dead??" I solemnly questioned.

"I don't think so, he appears to have a smile on his snout. I think if he were dead he wouldn't look so happy," my father joked.

Suddenly, Mr. Bundy appeared, and grabbed Chomper's leash dragging him off the hood of our car.

Chomper landed on his head but he didn't seem to mind. We cautiously got out of the car, and innocently asked Mr. Bundy "What happened to Chomper?".

However, he was too discombobulated to answer, and just mumbled as he dragged Chomper back to his yard and stuffed him into his dog house.

We scampered back up to my bedroom, and watched from my window as Chomper staggered around his dog house and even started chasing his tail around for a while.

Finally he just laid on the dirt and crashed for a few hours.

When the drug finally started to wear off, he slowly got up and started barking.

He was back to normal.

"Show Time!" my father exclaimed.

My father then sent me back into the basement lab, and ordered me to begin compounding mass quantities of LSD.

Chapter 9

My parents ultimately quit their jobs at the phone company, and were now taking orders and making deliveries of LSD all over Bakersfield, including all the local colleges and universities.

It was amazing that people were literally lining up at our backdoor, and that there was such a high demand for the drug that I was fabricating in our basement!

The incredible thing was, that at the time, LSD was not illegal, and my dad had no worries whatsoever about getting caught dealing the drug.

It wasn't until the IRS got involved, that my father got busted for tax evasion.

We had a great run for a few years, but when the IRS audited my father, they quickly put us out of business.

All the money my father made from selling LSD went down the tubes, paying for lawyers, taxes and interest owed.

My father also had to do some jail time.

Everyone thought it was excessive, throwing him into San Quentin with all those hardened criminals just for tax evasion.

Ten years seemed like forever but it could have been a lot worse.

It was a sad and scary day watching them take my father away from the courtroom.

Seconds after the judge slammed his gavel for the last time, US marshals swarmed him.

Maybe they thought he would try to make a break for the door or go after the judge.

He just stood there in a daze as they shackled him, and escorted him out of a side door.

We didn't even have a chance to say goodbye or anything to him.

He was gone, devoured by the California judicial system.

I personally don't know how he coped with being constrained. He was extremely claustrophobic. Being shackled, and then locked up in the back of a tiny US Marshal paddy wagon would have put him into a severe panic attack!

I've seen it happen once before, when an elevator door didn't open as expected.

We were at a department store, and an unfortunate delivery man was in the elevator with us. The elevator stopped but the door remained closed. My father's face became pale and sweat began pouring out of his entire body. I frantically began pushing the alarm button over and over, and prayed someone would open the door before my father turned into the Hulk!!

He was drenching up like a dry mop in a pail of soapy water!

In just those few seconds he looked as if he had fallen into a swimming pool, and was fighting to breathe as if he was being held underwater.

He was literally drowning in that stuck elevator, and he began screaming and clawing at its doors.

The delivery man began acting as a lifeguard, and tried to calm my father down.

"Relax sir, we are safe in here," he calmly stated.

Suddenly my father looked up and noticed a little trap door on the ceiling of the elevator.

Just as a drowning swimmer might attack the lifeguard who is trying to rescue him, my father frantically clawed his way up that poor delivery man to get up to that little escape hatch on the ceiling!

His world was spinning and he was suffocating!

He desperately needed to get out of there!

In his mind, he believed he was going to die.

I stayed clear out of his way as he managed to use that delivery man as a climbing pole, and then he desperately punched that trap door open with his fist!

He clung tightly to its framed opening as he dangled from the ceiling.

Just as he began frantically pulling himself up through the opening, the elevator began to move and the door magically opened!

My father instantly let go of the frame, and he came crashing down on top of that poor delivery man!

At that point, it was almost comical to see my dad laying on top of that poor guy with his packages strewn all about on the elevator floor, as they rolled around on top of each other.

People were curiously gawking in, believing that there must have been some sort of fight between my dad and the unconscious delivery man who was laying underneath him.

I quickly helped them up, and my father became a human again and apologized to the man.

I can only imagine the mess he must have made busting out of those shackles, and trying to break out of the back of that truck!

I hope he will survive jail time.

Chapter 10

While dad was incarcerated, my mother got her old job back (part time) at the phone company.

Though she insisted that I get back to work in my chemistry lab. We needed the money.

I had to continue making LSD, but now my mom was in charge of peddling it to pay the bills.

This time she was keeping financial records to make sure the IRS got their tax cut of our drug money.

However, in 1968, the government finally made LSD illegal, and I joyfully had to stop producing it.

Now I can put my energy into new projects.

For some extra money, I went back to making fireworks. Not the small cherry bombs I used to mess with, but large mortar fired skyrockets and quarter stick firecrackers which were equivalent to a 1/4 stick of dynamite.

Marco and I had some fun with those!

During that summer, I also began dabbling with chemical serums that could possibly boost muscle development.

Why, you might ask?

Not that I was scrawny or weak, but I used to read the advertisements in the back of my comic books. They were selling "secret elixirs" that could transform skinny, wimpy kids into heavyweight muscular bodybuilders.

So, finally, one day I decided to order that bodybuilding brew, and a few other items that all seemed legit.

All together it cost me less than 5 bucks, plus 2 dollars shipping.

To my disappointment, after I received the goods, the growth serum turned out to be just red Kool Aid.

I was so disgusted with myself that I was so naive that I got ripped off buying it.

I also discovered that the two other items I purchased from the comic book were also totally bogus.

X-Ray spec's were fake and didn't reveal any naked bodies, and Sea Monkeys were just baby brine shrimps swimming around in the water.

No shiny crowns, no funny tricks, no nothing.

I decided that if I was going to grow muscles, and impress Kelly Mosely, I had to invent my own muscle building serum.

I had to work quickly because summer was coming to an end, and we will be entering high school in a few weeks.

I was extremely excited about High school.

Not because of the chemistry and the science curriculum, but because of Kelly Mosely.

I've been enduring my middle school years dreaming about Kelly ever since we parted ways at the end of that fabulous summer.

Yearning for the day Kelly and I would at last be reunited in high school and return once again to my secret waterfall.

Together once and for all, and we could declare our unbridled love and passion for each other forever!

She too must be desperately anticipating our reunion.

Her father surely kept her tucked away from all the northy riff raff in our neighborhood, and she positively has been saving herself for only me.

Soon, we will be together my darling, in the same school and in love.

I've been dreaming about being together with her, biding my time, anticipating our forever lasting love to come.

I really have to get started on my body building serum! I've been doing some research, and I needed to acquire some specific growth hormones to experiment with.

Since I couldn't get my hands on any human brains to dissect and make my extractions, I needed to find the next best thing, some animal brains to dissect.

I convinced my mother to drive Marco and I to a meat packing plant on the other side of town for some of the materials I needed.

It was a seedy area and the air reeked of death.

Big metal tubular pens, imprisoned several unlucky, filthy manure covered animals, who were just mucking about, and clueless of their upcoming unfortunate demise.

They were just minding their own business, chewing on urine drenched hay, while unexpectedly awaiting their turn to be shot or bludgeoned to death, and then get strung up only to be pieced out for someone's dinner plate.

There weren't just cows that were muddling around. Dozens of pigs, goats and sheep were penned in there too.

I also noticed a lonely deer chained up to a tree. Poor Bambi, awaiting some wealthy hunter to sneak up and shoot him while chained up to that tree.

My mother waited in the car as Marco and I walked up to the main office of the packing plant.

"Why do they call a slaughter house a meat packing plant?" Marco asked.

"I don't know, maybe because they pack the animals into little convenient packages so they don't resemble what they once were," I replied.

We entered the office, and we were surrounded by numerous posters of all sorts of meat products behind a tall counter. The room was filled with cigar smoke coming from a large husky man who was sitting at his desk, and going over some invoices.

I noticed a thin layer of saw dust cast over the floor, presumably to soak up any blood that might be tracked in from the kill room.

The man peered up at us looking over his glasses as we entered the office, but didn't bother getting up, since he knew we were probably not there to buy anything.

After a minute or two he reluctantly stood up, and his chair screeched and rolled away from him.

He walked over to the counter where we were standing.

"He sure does look like an animal murderer to me," whispered Marco.

His face was hard and he had a stern look about him.

It was apparent that he must be the executioner.

The animal hitman who has no conscience or problem slitting a pig's throat or chopping off a chicken's head while he binds its feet together with his free hand. Oddly, I noticed he had a little dog running between his feet.

I wondered if that little dog knew that he was living with an animal serial killer.

"What do you boys want?" he gruffed.

"Sir, I am wondering if we may be able to obtain some cow brains for some scientific experiments I am composing?" I asked.

"You want to buy some cow brains? Those are going to cost you kid. I sell those for $2.95 a pound," he stated.

"People actually buy that stuff to eat?!" I gasped.

"Haven't you ever heard of 'cervelle de veau' kid? That's cow brains," he smugly replied.

"Is there anything here we can get for free?" Marco interjected.

The man directed us to the backyard area, behind the kill room building.

He informed us that there would be a large open trailer filled with animal remnants that we could look through.

He gave us a large burlap sack, and sent us on our way.

I was getting excited to be able to acquire some specimens for my experiment, but when we arrived at the trailer, it was the grossest smelling, most disgusting site I had ever seen.

The trailer was filled to the brim with dozens upon dozens of mortified animal heads, guts, and other useless body parts.

"Dig in," joked Marco.

I held my breath and squinted my eyes as I grabbed a large sheep head by the horns and dropped it into the sack.

Next I went for a pig head, and finally a goat head which also had handle like horns attached to it.

"How about a few chicken heads, Buck Buck?" Marco clucked.

There were several cow heads in the pile, but their skulls were already cracked open and their brains removed.

The trailer was so disgusting, we ran back to the car as fast as we could, dragging the bloody sack behind us.

We threw the sack in the trunk and hopped back into the car.

"Did you get what you needed?" my mother asked.

"I hope so," replied Marco.

When we returned home, Marco helped me remove the brains from the skulls by using a small hatchet we had in the garage and his Italian switchblade that his father had given him.

He was outside chopping away as I searched for some plastic freezer bags.

He placed the brains in a bucket and I asked him what he had done with the empty heads?

"I threw them away," he smirked.

I placed the brains into our basement freezer, and then Marco and I decided to take it easy and watch an episode of "Combat," our favorite TV show.

It was difficult trying to erase those ghastly images of the death bin trailer, so what better than to watch a bunch of Nazi's getting blown to pieces by hand grenades to cleanse our minds.

A short time later, as we were still watching television, we heard a loud shriek coming from down the street.

"Gee, that sounded like old lady Bugnacki!" I stated as we kept our attention tuned in on the TV and ate popcorn as the Nazis were getting obliterated.

"I guess she must have found those busted up animal heads I tossed into her garbage can!" Marco laughed.

Marco then asked if he could use the phone to call his step mother.

His parents had been divorced about six years ago. Apparently Mr. Delgato threatened to kill his mother if she tried to get custody of Marco.

She must have believed him because she left Marco with his dad, and she returned to Italy for her safety.

I heard him asking his step mother if his father was home, and if I could come over for dinner.

"Hey Donny, put your shoes on, you're coming to my house for dinner.

You're going to have real Italian food tonight!" he boasted.

"Hey mom, can I go to Marco's for some real Italian food for supper?" I begged.

"What do you mean "Real" Italian food? I cook real Italian food all the time! Chef Boyardee is real Italian food!" she exclaimed.

I raised my eyebrows and she realized that maybe this might be a little different.

"Well…Okay go ahead," she reluctantly replied.

Chapter 11

Marco and I left my house, and we followed the path through the woods to Marco's house.

His father wasn't home, but his step mother was in the kitchen wearing skin tight red spandex pants, a yellow halter top, and tall black spike high heeled stiletto shoes. Not that I was paying much attention to her.

She was originally from New York City, and she had a very heavy Brooklyn accent.

Mrs. Delgato, who was in her mid thirties wasn't very pretty, but she had an exotic look about her that screamed "I'm horny all the time!" that made up for it.

She had a bonafide killer body, and her hair was big, poufy and bleached blond.

She wore long gold tone "cat claw" press on fingernails and long black fake eyelashes that always seemed ready to fall off.

Her bright red lipstick outlined her thick full lips which Marco referred to as "Beacho lips".

I didn't exactly know what "Beacho lips" were, until I met her, then I understood.

She usually dressed very trashy, and Marco informed me that most of the time she parades around the house only wearing a tiny pink satin robe!

She had always been nice to me, but in a flirty manner.

"Hoy Doawnny. So glad ya could make it for Dinna! We're havin Scungilli tonight! Marco's favo-rite! I hope you are hungray," she whined.

"Yes, I am, thank you. But I don't know what Scungilli is?" I replied.

"Let's just say it's seafood," she chuckled.

Marco tugged me and urged me to follow him upstairs to his room, and he shut and dead bolted the door.

"Hey check these out!" he gloated.

He dragged out a large cardboard box of comic books that were hidden in the back of his closet.

"I really don't feel like reading comic books," I stated.

"These ones you will," he replied.

The comic book on top was an old Archie comic that looked like it had been read a hundred and one times. Marco removed it from the box, and tossed it on the floor. What laid beneath was the Holy Grail of all teenage boys' dreams. A tall stack of about 50 raunchy adult magazines!

I instantly grabbed one, and began flipping through the pages!

"Geez, these pictures are disgusting! I love this stuff!" I excitedly whispered.

"I've seen the Playboys that my father had stashed in his closet, but these pictures made my dad's playboys look like 'Time Magazine!'" I exclaimed.

Marco was searching through the stack looking for something specific.

"There's something in here I want to show you," he whispered.

Then he found it, and pulled out an abused magazine, and began flipping through its pages.

"Here it is! Check this out!" he exclaimed.

I was almost afraid to look, but I had to see what he was talking about.

I took the magazine, and what I saw corrupted my brain for the rest of my adolescent life!

My innocence was crushed, killed, destroyed, and I'll never be able to see again!

The pictures were lewd, explicit and obscene, and the woman featured in all those pictures was so raunchy, crude and erotically filthy. I was stunned and I couldn't take my eyes off of them!

Those perverted acts with all those men and farm animals were probably illegal in every country, except France!

"Where did you find these magazines!" I exclaimed.

"I didn't find them. They were given to me by someone who lives here!" Marco coyly replied.

"Holy Shit! I can't believe your mother would allow your dad to have this filthy smut in your house, and then he gave them to you!

I wish my dad was that cool!" I exclaimed.

"Oh yeah wise guy, take a closer look at that hot blond right there...look closer, that's my stepmom performing those disgusting sex acts in these pictures, and these were her magazines! She gave them to me!" he bragged.

That was way too much information for my feeble teenage mind to process!

My body began to heat up and my testosterone level was red lining and about to explode!!

My heart began to pound like war drums just prior to Custer's last stand!

That slut machine of a woman in the magazine was downstairs making my Scungilli!

"Doesn't it freak you out to see your step mom in this magazine?!" I asked.

"It used to be a little weird, but I got more comfortable with it after she asked me to start taking showers with her to save water! She also gave me a few of the movies that she performed in too. Maybe we'll watch them sometimes when nobody is around," he stated.

Now, I finally realized how disturbed and demented Marco's family really was!

"Marco...please! Can I live here with you???!" I begged and pleaded and begged some more.

Chapter 12

"Boyz! Come and geeedd it!" Mrs. D's voice called from downstairs.

"I instantly pondered, how many other times has she uttered those very same words..."Boyz, come and get it!".

Marco returned the magazines into the box and placed the Archie comic on the top, before closing the box and placing it back into his closet.

I didn't understand why he had that Archie comic on top, maybe he didn't want his father knowing what was going on around there while he wasn't around.

We rushed down stairs (well I rushed), and sat down at the dining room table, and now Mrs. Delgato had taken on a new light to me.

I watched her as she was busy getting dinner ready. Squatting up and down as she looked into the oven. Peeling and eating a Banana. Shaking up a can of whipped cream! I was going crazy!

I couldn't get those perverted images of her out of my mind!

Just then I heard a car pull into the driveway, and a car door squeaked open, and then slammed closed. A moment later Mr. Delgato came storming in.

"What's fa Dinner! I'm starvin!" he exclaimed.

Just then he noticed me sitting in his seat at the table.

"Hey punk...Minga, get outa my chair!" he barked.

I was so startled, I fell off the chair and hit the floor.

They all began laughing.

"He's just kidding with you Donny!" laughed Marco.

I picked myself up and sat in a different chair as Mr. D sat down next to me.

I was so intimidated by him. I could hardly breath.

"So Donny, Marco tells me you are pretty good wid makin' bombs. Do ya think youz can make me one dat could blow open a safe? Der's a bank downtown dat I'm think'in about make'in a withdrawl from," he joked.

"Very funny Daaad," Marco chuckled.

"Okay, howz about a car bomb? Can yaz make somethin dat'le blow up a car!?" inquired Mr. Delgato.

"Dad!!" exclaimed Marco.

"Sure thing Mr. D," I sarcastically mumbled as I sat at their table watching luscious Mrs. D parading around the kitchen.

Damn, I wish I had brought my X-Ray specs!

Finally, plates were passed out and a big bowl of linguini with some sort of orangey meat pieces were placed on the table. It was followed up with a large loaf of Italian bread, salad and some canned mushy green beans.

Mrs. D leaned over me, rubbing her chest against me as she used a large pasta fork, and plopped a huge pile of the scungilli on my plate.

She continued servicing...I mean serving everyone else, as I sat there staring at my Scungilli.

"Hey kid, have you ever eat'n Scungilli before?" Mr. Delgato asked.

"No sir, actually I don't know what it is," I replied.

"It's a big slimy sea snail, now dig in!" he laughed.

Did he just say a "sea snail"? I picked up my fork and inconspicuously pushed the orange meat to the side and nibbled at the linguini.

"Hey! I don't see youz eatin' the Scungilli!" shouted Mr. Delgato.

I began to panic because there was no way my teeth would allow that sea snail to enter my mouth!

"I don't think I like Scungilli sir," I nervously replied.

"Did youz ever try Scungilli?" he asked.

"No sir, I haven't," I replied back.

"So howz do ya knowz youz don't like it, if youz never eaten it? Youz should try it! Try it, and youz might like it," he declared.

I nodded my head in agreement.

How did I know I didn't like it, if I never tried it?

The problem was, it was sooo gross!

But it seemed that I had no choice.

It was either eat it, or die in the river wearing cement boots.

I stabbed a tiny morsel of slimy snail meat as everyone at the table watched.

I slowly raised the fork, and struggled to open my mouth. I scraped the rubbery orange tidbit off the fork with my front tooth, and I reluctantly chewed the rubbery meat with my front teeth.

Everyone was silently waiting for my response as I swallowed the slimy mollusk.

Suddenly my eyes lit up and I became excited!

"I like orange Scungilli! I like it here! I like it there! I like it, I like it everywhere!!" I joked impersonating Dr. Seuss.

"Oh a wise guy, huh?" stated Mr. Delgato.

Scungilli was actually pretty good, and I even asked for a second helping.

Marco and I helped clean up after dinner, and I thanked Mrs. Delgato for dinner as she was hand washing the dishes.

Now it appeared to me that whatever she was doing, it was erotic to me.

I still felt a huge load of testosterone in my stomach. The ecstasy of seeing Mrs. D in that magazine... I couldn't get those perverted images out of my mind!

And now she was right in front of me, with all that carnal knowledge packed away in her tiny brain!

"That was really good Mrs. D, but I don't think my mom will ever make that for me," I sadly stated.

Then, I suddenly noticed that we were all alone in the kitchen.

Marco and his father had disappeared.

She stopped washing the dishes and stared deeply into my eyes, and seductively careened over to me.

Then she embraced me with her soaking wet dish suds arms.

Not just a hug, but pressing her body into me, melding us together, and smearing white bubble foam all over me! She softly nibbled my ear with her "Beacho lips" as she continued grinding her steaming hot body against mine!

I could still smell the Scungilli on her breath but I didn't care.

"If you want some more Scungilli, you should com ova when no one is around, and I will make it with ya," she erotically stated and she pressed her lips against mine and began passionately making out with me! Tongue and everything!

For a brief moment I envisioned where her mouth had once been in those magazine pictures, but at that point I didn't care what sort of diseases she might be harboring!

"Donny! Donny!" I heard a voice coming from a tin can.

Marco began shaking my arm, and he abruptly snapped me out of my "Mrs. D porno daydream"!

"What are you spacing out about!" he demanded.

"Um, uhh…science stuff?" was my quick response.

"Oooh, I know what you was dreamin' about…," he smirked. And then he glanced at his step mom as she was vigorously plunging out a tall glass with a long handled tube brush over the kitchen sink.

"Shit was I that obvious!" I thought.

I turned bright red out of embarrassment, and hightailed it towards the front door!

"Oh my it's so late, I have to get home!" I exclaimed.

"Thank you Mrs. D! You are really great in the kitchen!" I blurted out as I was rushing towards the door.

Geez, did I just say that! What an idiot I am!

"Ya wellllcome, don't be a stranga!" she laughed.

And she blew me a kiss as I ran out the front door!

Chapter 13

I worked day and night experimenting with different brain enzymes, hormones and chemicals.

Then I finally came across a solution that could quadruple the muscle mass of a rat with just one injection.

But, I needed a larger specimen to experiment my formula on. I instantly thought of my go to guinea pig dog, Chomper.

The only issue was that I had to inject the drug, and there was no way I could get close enough to him to do that.

So I fabricated a dart out of a syringe.

I glued on arrow feathers, and a lead fishing sinker taped onto the top of the plunger.

I then attached a fine stretch of fishing line to it and I found a long copper pipe in the garage that the syringe fit perfectly into.

I loaded the dart into the pipe.

Then, from my bedroom window, I waited for Chomper to crawl out of his dog house.

I made several "Meow" sounds over and over and it didn't take long for Chomper to hear me.

He curiously came prowling out of his dog house, aggressively sniffing for the unfortunate feline.

I nervously raised my blow pipe and blasted a burst of hot air as hard as I could.

The dart blasted from the tube and spiraled through the air and stuck him right in the back of Chompers neck!

That was a one in a million shot, and I doubted that I could hit that mark twice in a row!

Chomper gave out a yelp, which was odd coming from that ferocious beast, and he began shaking his head furiously trying to remove the dart.

I quickly pulled the line, and jerked the syringe back over the fence and back up into my room.

Then I anxiously sat and watched from my bedroom window as Chomper began walking around in tiny circles. After a few minutes, he finally stopped and began shaking uncontrollably.

His jet black fur instantly began fading and his face turned totally gray! The skin around his mouth and eyes began to swell and droop, and he began slumping over as if he had aged approximately ten years! That's seventy years in dog years. And then he suddenly began urinating all over himself as he rolled over on the ground!

His muscles didn't grow, but his metabolism was jolted forward, and he seemed to rapidly age in a matter of minutes!

I panicked when I heard Mr. Bundy coming out of the house with Chomper's dinner.

I quickly closed my window and hid behind the shades.

"What da hell did you get into? White paint?!" Mr. Bundy shouted at his dog.

He dragged a limp Chomper to the garden hose, and vigorously tried washing out all the gray from Chompers' once jet black coat.

All Chomper could do was just lay there in the mud, and occasionally let out a squirt of urine, and then he finally crapped all over himself!

Mr. Bundy dragged him back to his dog house and then went back inside scratching his head.

I continued watching Chomper, and every few hours I peeked out my window, and checked to see if the serum had worn off yet, and if Chomper had been restored to his youthful vicious self.

But there were no changes, and he still appeared to be an old bag of dog bones.

I went to bed pondering the situation, maybe it'll take a little time and by morning Chomper will be back to normal.

After that massive geriatric transformation, I decided that it was way too risky messing with hormones and chemical isotopes to increase my body mass, especially after seeing what had happened to Chomper.

Kelly Mosely will just have to accept me for who I am. A 95 pound lean, mean science machine!

When I awoke the following morning, I quickly sprang out of bed, and looked out my window to see if Chomper had returned to his normal self.

But sadly, he was just laying there, peeing all over himself and still looking like an old great great grand-dog.

I guess I'll just have to classify this as irreversible chemically induced geriatric disfigurement, and slip that chemical formula into my "Whoops" box.

I wrote a detailed letter to my dad about it, and I told him that my experiment proved one thing…

"You can't teach an old dog new tricks. But I can make a young dog turn into an old trick!".

Chapter 14

Summer finally came to an end, and school was about to begin.

The first day of high school is today, and I can't wait to sweep "my future bride to be" off her feet!

I awoke to the smell of sizzling bacon and eggs.

Usually I would have dreaded the first day of high school but I've been biding my time for the past three years, and eagerly anticipating my reunion with my destiny and soul mate Kelly Mosely.

She's probably as eager for our reunion as I am, and today is the day!

As I waited for the bus at the end of my driveway, I couldn't help but be a little bit nervous.

"What if Kelly forgot about me? What if she thinks I'm a skinny nerd!?" I could be doomed, I thought.

Then I saw a big yellow school bus charging down the street toward me, and it abruptly stopped right in front of me, almost running me over.

The driver opened up the door and I quickly moved to enter the bus.

As I hurried to step up, the driver quickly slammed the door closed before I had a chance to stop, and I crashed into the closed door, slamming my forehead against it.

I was dazed and my head was throbbing, and then the door reopened.

I could hear all the kids laughing along with my nemesis "Dwain the insane" bus driver.

He repeated that process, opening and closing the bi-fold bus door several times, until he finally let me on board.

"Real funny Dwain, I'm surprised they gave you your job back after all those DUI's you were busted for," I taunted.

"They weren't all DUI's smart ass. I'm also a certified JSP…Juvenile Sex Predator," he snickered.

I continued down the aisle to find a seat, and I ran through the usual gauntlet of north end trouble makers as I was making my way down the narrow aisle to find a seat.

I was tripped, punched, hit with spitballs, and finally pushed into a seat that had vomit on it.

"Great way to start high school," I thought.

Spitballs in my hair and puke on the seat of my pants.

I spied around the bus, but I didn't see Kelly.

The usual riff raff from the north end of my street was on the bus, but no Kelly.

"Hmmm, maybe her father is bringing her to school or maybe she was out sick today. I'll have to look for her when I get to school," I thought.

The school bus rapidly turned into the high school parking lot, and screeched to an abrupt stop in front of the school. Dwain flung the door open, and sang:

"The first day of school is the worst day of school and the last day of school is the best day of school!" and then he laughed.

"Welcome to hell!" was his jovial final comment.

I was hastily leaving the bus, and stepping down the steps,

when Duane kicked me from behind and I was launched off the bus and landed hard on the pavement below.

My pencils and binders went flying all over the place, and I was struggling to pick them up.

That's when I heard a loud car enter the school's parking lot, backfiring and blowing black smoke from its rusty exhaust pipes.

At a glance I knew that it was Kenny Johnson's car. I had seen him racing up and down our street all summer with his green hunk of junk Ford Woody Wagon hot rod, that he scraped together from parts he found at the junkyard.

Actually, I was surprised that he was still in high school, he stayed back a few times, and he was certainly old enough at eighteen to drop out.

I oddly noticed the head of a small girl bobbing around in the car with him as his car bucked through the parking lot.

"What sort of girl in her right mind would be his girlfriend?". It was baffling.

Personally, it would totally gross me out having his "hairy ass" skinned hand roaming all over my body!

But, my curiosity got the better of me, so I waited and watched as his car jerked and lurched into its final resting place.

It let out a loud "Bang!" as his car backfired when he shut off its engine.

But, I still couldn't identify who the girl was that was with him, since they were grossly making out, and pawing all over each other in the front seat of his hunk a junk car.

Blaahhh, disgusting and cringe worthy!

Making out with Kenny would be worse than licking a petri dish of dog stool infested with hookworms!

Realizing they were going to be late, Kenny suddenly jumped out of the car, and ran around to open the door for his girlfriend.

Her small head began to rise up, and her light brunette hair blew in the wind as she stepped out of the car and turned toward me.

It suddenly felt as if a race horse had just kicked me in the stomach and then I was run over and dragged down the street by a garbage truck!

I was mortified as I watched "Butt-r-fingers" assist my future wife, Kelly Mosely out of his piece of shit Woody!

I instantly became nauseous and delirious.

I couldn't breath as I staggered there, fighting gravity to keep from collapsing and I began searching my pockets for a syringe full of epinephrine to stab directly into my heart!

I was in a state of paralysis, as the two lovebirds strolled toward me.

"Hello Donny Lord," Kelly coolly stated.

All I could do was faintly flip up my fingers in an attempt to acknowledge her.

"Hi, Kelly" I squeaked out.

Kenny smugly smirked at me as he clutched Kelly close to him, as they strutted past me.

I don't know why I said what I did, but it came out of nowhere. Maybe I was so frustrated to see Kenny with Kelly under his arm.

"Welcome back again to the tenth grade Butt-r-fingers," I jeered.

At that moment it seemed as if all the traffic had screeched to an abrupt stop! All the kids walking toward the building became catatonic and turned towards us.

Even the birds flying overhead froze in mid flight and peered down on us.

No one could believe what I had just said to Kenny, and my life was about to end.

Kenny's face became red and distorted as he began to grind his teeth.

"What did you say to me, schoolboy?!" he growled.

Just then Kelly interjected, possibly trying to save my life.

"Hey Donny, when is your dad getting out of Jail?" she quickly inquired.

"Uhm...In, in eight years," I stammered.

"Maybe you can hook us up with some free 'LSD,' and Kenny won't have to beat you up," she stated.

Kenny suddenly realized that I might be more valuable alive to him than dead, and he slowly dropped his clenched fists.

"Well, um, I stopped making that stuff since it became illegal," I replied.

"Ohh, that's too bad. Go ahead Kenny, you can kill him now," Kelly half heartedly stated.

Kenny began raising his hairy ass fist again, and drew back his arm, cocking it into the knockout position.

"But, But, But!!" I stammered.

Kenny became extremely agitated and more enraged as he heard me repeat..."Butt, Butt, Butt!", and then he launched his fist into the side of my face, violently knocking me down to the ground!

My books and notebook papers once again flew everywhere, as Kenny and Kelly casually stepped over me.

Until now, I never really believed that Wylie Coyote saw "stars" encircling his head after he was knocked out by a falling rock, or run over by a truck.

For the first time in my life, I actually saw stars and planets revolving around my head!

Embarrassed and humiliated, I slowly got up, gathered my things and made my way into the school.

What a dreadful way to start off the first day of school. After wandering the halls, I finally found my home room and dizzily staggered in.

The whole class was silent as they gazed upon the massive, inflamed red hematoma Kenny had bestowed upon my face, along with spit balls in my hair and vomit on the seat of my pants.

I quickly found my chair, and plopped myself down into my seat.

As I glanced around the room, I instantly realized that sitting two seats behind me was Kelly Mosely, and next to her holding her hand with his hairy ass hand, was Kenny Johnson!

The classrooms were organized alphabetically "Johnson, Lord and Mosley," J-L and M.

Kelly just sat there chewing her gum like a cow, and cracking bubbles in her mouth, as they both whispered and giggled back and forth with each other.

My whole image of Kelly was swept away in a raging tidal wave, and flushed down the toilet into the cesspool of unkind love.

Kelly was a tainted Northie now, and I was a Southie. We could never be together after she made out with Butt-r-fingers Johnson. And now, she was his girlfriend.

I certainly don't want her anymore...never! ...Well at least till the end of the day.

Unfortunately, Kenny's deplorable influence had turned Kelly into a low life druggie like himself and all the others they associate with.

And so it went, from that day on, each and every morning, Kenny and Kelly were standing there, waiting for me in front of the school, tormenting me for drugs.

Because I would consistently refuse and say "No!", I would get a vicious punch in the face that always knocked me down, courtesy of Kenny.

This went on for several weeks until I finally had enough and stood up for myself...

I think it's time to bring my best friend Marco Delgato into this situation.

Chapter 15

I invited Marco over to my house the following weekend, and we blew up some old pumpkins that were growing in Mr. Bundy's garden.

"So Donny, it's been a while and I haven't seen you since school started, how is High school going? Did you finally hook up with Kelly Mosely?" he inquired.

I didn't want to come right out and complain about Kenny beating me up every day, so I meandered around his question.

"Well, things are not going so good," I replied.

"Whaz a matter!" he exclaimed and was deeply concerned.

"Well Marco, the bad news is that Kelly has been going out with Kenny Johnson. I saw them making out in his car the first day of school, and as sick as it sounds they are together," I sadly stated.

"Minga! She is with Butt-fingers! She is garbage if she is with that piece of crap! You don't need that headache!" Marco exclaimed.

"By the way, what happened to your face? How did you get that nasty bruise on it?" Marco inquired.

"Awe it's nothing, I walked into a door," I half heartedly replied.

"A door?!" Marco questioned, as he made a puzzled face. He began to give me the cold stare as he studied my contusion.

"You know I once hit a kid so hard, I knocked his teeth right through the side of his cheek," Marco bragged.

"That bruise looks like you got belted! Who did that to you?!" he demanded to know.

"Well, Kenny has been giving me a hard time for the past few weeks. Kelly wants me to make LSD for them and Kenny has been trying to force me to do it by bullying me every day.

He punched me in the face the first day of school, and almost knocked me out. It was the first time I ever saw stars floating around my head.

He has been after me every morning since then, threatening me that I had better make the drug for them. And, when I refuse to do it, I get punched in the face each morning. Maybe I'll go talk to the vice principal about it on Monday," I sadly stated.

"He did that to you!!" Marco exclaimed.

"Yes, but sometimes it's not too bad and I don't always see the stars," I softly replied.

"Don't do anything on Monday…I wanna talk to Kenny about it," Marco sternly stated.

"Marco, don't do anything crazy, okay," I half heartedly insisted.

"Don't you worry about it," Marco replied.

He picked up a large pumpkin by its stem, and started walking away with it.

I watched him make a fist and violently punch a hole clean through the pumpkin!

Then he tossed it back into Mr. Bundy's garden and continued walking home with his fists clenched.

I slept so good that night!

My troubles will soon be over!

My only concern was that Marco might not get there in time on Monday morning to save me, or he could totally forget about it.

I might just have one more incident with Kenny.

I could just stay home from school Monday morning, but I didn't want to chance it and miss out if Marco does show up. I wanted to be there to watch Kenny get murdered. It was a chance I had to take.

Chapter 16

It was cloudy and raining out that Monday morning.

My mother always says "It's a good day to go to school when it's raining".

I never understood the logic behind that since Kenny didn't care if it was raining or not when he beat me up as Kelly stood by, and cheered him on.

"Ya know what Mom, the sun is coming out, and it is going to be a good day to go to school today!" I exclaimed.

I believed that if Marco came through, Kenny was hopefully going to have a very bad day today.

I eagerly gulped down my breakfast, and ran to meet the bus at the end of my driveway.

When the bus finally arrived, I hesitated as Dwain opened, and closed the door several times before he allowed me on.

I found a seat near the back of the bus next to Crystal Mckune. She was a geeky redheaded girl, who possibly was as much of a nerd as me, but not nearly as smart.

It was difficult to get past her frazzled dark red hair, full braces with the cervical pull orthodontic overbite headgear, and cat eye glasses.

Although I think someday she might just blossom, and become a very beautiful woman, but for now, not so much.

She was always nice to me though, and I think she understood the grueling punishment I was constantly getting dished out from Kenny.

Then some of the kids on the bus began taunting me about Kenny.

Apparently he was bragging over the weekend that he was going to kill me this morning, because Kelly really wanted to get some LSD out of me!

"If I were you Lord…I wouldn't get off the bus today!" one kid shouted.

I just sank into my seat, and prayed as Crystal gave me a sad look of remorse.

The bus finally pulled into the school parking lot, and I noticed Kenny standing next to his car making out with Kelly.

They were grossly slobbering all over each other for the entire world to see.

It was sickening. Why was she with that loser? I really couldn't understand it. She must have the same thing wrong with her as Mrs. Bundy!

I thought I might just have a chance to sneak into school, since Kenny seemed to be preoccupied, so I quickly gathered my things and rushed off the bus.

I actually thought I was going to make it, until Dwain suddenly slammed the folding door shut before I could get off!

"What's your hurry Lord?" he snickered.

I frantically reached over and pulled the door release lever myself and jumped off the bus!

I was running for the school's large entry doors, when I heard my name shouted out from behind me!

"Hey! Lord!!" I recognized Kenny's voice and quickly grabbed the handle of the door!

"Phew, I just made it!!" I exclaimed to myself!

Then I felt a hard claw grab me by the shoulder, and I was quickly pulled around!

What felt like a rock, hit me on the side of my face, and then again in my eye!

I fell to the ground as the stars once again began circling around my head. Kenny laughed, and stepped over me as he continued into the building.

I vaguely saw Kelly following behind him, and then I felt a hard kick to my stomach, as I laid incapacitated on the ground! My soul mate just kicked me as hard as she could!

"You better get us the dope, school boy!" she angrily scoffed.

I couldn't believe it.

The girl I was in love with, wasn't even close to what I ever imagined anymore.

I heard the school bell ring, and then I felt a soft hand touch my shoulder, and helped me up. It was Crystal.

"Are you okay, Donny?" she softly asked.

I slowly climbed to my feet, and saw in her face that something was wrong.

"What is it!" I demanded.

"I think you better go to the nurse...your eye is black and there is blood in it.

Also there is a huge red bruise on the side of your face," she stated with concern.

I gathered my things, and rushed into the nearest boy's lavatory.

As I faced myself in the mirror, my skull was still pounding. My eye was full of blood, and the skin around it was turning black.

There was an imprint of Kenny's knuckles on my cheek, and it was turning from red to blue.

I washed my face, and held a cold wet paper towel over my eye. I probably should have gone to the nurse, but I didn't want to have to tell the principal what happened.

If I ratted out Kenny, it would be worse and everyone would call me a "rat fink".

I hid in a stall of the boy's lavatory soaking my bloody black eye all morning, until I finally heard the noon lunch bell ring.

"I have to get out of here, what if Kenny comes in here and finds me," I thought.

I quickly ducked out a side door and left school, and I began walking home.

"What the hell happened to Marco!" I thought to myself as I wavered down the street.

I found an old beer can lying on the edge of the sidewalk, and began kicking it down the walk.

As I turned the corner I noticed a large boy heading toward me.

It was difficult to see him through my bloody eye as I clutched my stomach, and held the wet paper towel on my face. But the boy seemed to recognize me, and came racing toward me...It was Marco!

"What happened ta you!!!" he shouted.

"Kenny sucker punched me, and Kelly gave me a hard kick in the stomach for good measure," I moaned.

I didn't see any reason to protect her after what she had done to me.

"Come on! We're going back to school!" he firmly ordered.

"No! I don't want to go back there looking like this," I groaned.

"You look a lot better now than what Kenny is going to look like when I'm done with him!" Marco exclaimed.

I shrugged my shoulders and I reluctantly turned back, and we briskly returned to my school.

Chapter 17

As we entered the school building, Marco ordered me to go to my class, and he would find me later.

I wandered off on my own, down the empty hallways, as Marco went into one of the boy's lavatories.

I could hear the loud crashing of a metal trash can getting smashed to pieces, as Marco unleashed his rage on it.

I rushed into my classroom and quickly found my seat, when my teacher asked where I had been all day? Really?

The whole school was talking about what had happened to me that morning, and she knew that I was most likely hiding out, or in the hospital.

Kenny was sitting in the back of the room smugly eyeing me, quite proud of what they had done to me that morning as he winked at Kelly, and gave her a "High Five" as they laughed about it.

Suddenly we heard a distant classroom door open aggressively, and Marco's loud voice echoing from the very first classroom down the hallway.

"Is Kenny Johnson in here?!!" he angrily shouted.

Then there was a pause, and the door was slammed shut!

This repeated over and over, all the way down the hallway, becoming louder as Marco worked his way through each classroom towards us!

A classroom door aggressively opened. Then Marco's loud angry voice repeating himself every few seconds,

"Is Kenny Johnson in here?!!", and then the door slammed shut!

Marco was vengefully on the hunt for Kenny Johnson. Rapidly making his way towards him room by room! As each door was opened and slammed shut, he became a step close to his prey!

Oddly not one teacher, not even the principal interfered with him.

As far as they were concerned, Kenny was going to get what was coming to him.

I looked over my shoulder, and noticed Kenny turning pale and the look of concern was creeping over him.

We heard Marco's angry voice getting louder and louder, and closer and closer to our classroom until he was finally right next door!

"Is Kenny Johnson in here!!" the voice angrily shouted from next door.

Kenny began sweating profusely, his face was bright red and the hairs on his ass hand began to stand straight up! He sank down into his seat, and prayed that he would be unnoticed and that no one would give him up.

Just then our classroom door barged open, and Marco was brazenly standing in the doorway with his fists clenched, and his face full of rage!

"Is Kenny Johnson in here!" he demanded.

Just then every kid in the classroom turned towards Kenny and Kelly, and pointed directly at them as they both sunk down into their chairs.

Marco quickly pushed the desks and chairs aside as he made his way toward Kenny.

Just as Marco was preparing to grab Kenny by the throat, Mr. Greasebank, the school's assistant principal came rushing in, and got in between them!

"It's not going to happen on my watch!" shouted Mr. Greasebank, and he pushed Marco back.

Marco looked around the room, and realized that it would be much better to kill Kenny in a more private place.

He coldly stared at Kenny and pointed his finger at his face.

"I will be waiting for you after school "Butt-r-finger!"

Be at the abandoned cement factory across the street at 2:30 or I'll come to your house, and beat the shit out of you, and your little brother Ricky Dicky!" Marco demanded.

He turned his deadly fixation, and pointed at Kelly,

"You come too!" he growled, and then he turned and walked out the door.

All the kids began to roar and chant!

"KENNY IS A DEAD MAN!! KENNY IS A DEAD MAN!! KENNY IS A DEAD MAN!!".

Kenny tried to be cool, and slowly struggled to lift himself up out of his wet seat.

His hair and clothes were soaked with perspiration.

When he finally made it to his feet, he wobbled between the scrambled maze of desks and chairs toward the classroom door as Kelly wavered next to him, propping him up so he wouldn't collapse.

The chanting continued:

"KENNY IS A DEAD MAN!!KENNY IS A DEAD MAN!!" over and over as he staggered out of the classroom, as though he was heading for the gallows and preparing for his life to end.

He unexpectedly stopped in the doorway and he turned back towards me, and just stared back at me with a desperate look of despair.

For the first time in my life, I think I actually saw what someone looked like when they knew they were going to die.

I think he was asking me for help.

He knew Marco came looking for him because of me, and he hoped I might show some sort of clemency toward him.

I turned away, and they left the room with Mr. Greasebank right behind them.

No one knew where they were going.

There were still two hours of school left, but rumors started flying that Kenny and Kelly were seen sneaking out of school.

They raced off in Kenny's heap, probably heading to Mexico to escape from Marco. One thing for sure, everyone doubted Kenny would ever show up.

Chapter 18

Those last two hours of school seemed to take forever.

The whole school population was on alert and planning to attend "The murder of Kenny Johnson".

It wasn't until the final bell rang that everyone vigorously poured out of the school building, and marched down the street to the old abandoned cement factory.

The school buses sat idle and empty as most of the kids followed the crowd to the empty factory parking lot.

I felt scared and anxious.

I had a nauseous, ache in my stomach that maybe something might go wrong and Marco could get hurt, but then I remembered it was Marco that Kenny had to deal with.

As I approached the factory I could see the rusty and deteriorated chain link fence which surrounded the old facility.

Hundreds of kids were pouring through the broken fence segments, and making their way into the factory's parking lot.

I could see Marco standing in the middle of the lot, surrounded on three sides by a staggered wall of large concrete blocks.

Kids were climbing up, and sitting on them, jockeying for the best seats in the house to view the fight of the century.

Marco stood there in a gladiator-like state of ferocity.

His fists clenched, with his brutal facial expression to commit supreme barbarity on to his enemy.

Even though he was there because of me, I was apprehensive about going over to see him. I didn't want to mess with his pre fight Mojo.

I just blended in with the crowd of blood thirsty spectators, as kids were betting on the duration of time Kenny would last before "Kenny was a dead man". The odds favored Marco that Kenny wouldn't last for a minute. In fact there were some bets going for under 30 seconds.

I personally don't think Kenny will last 15 seconds the way Marco is riled up.

It was 2:25 PM, and no Kenny yet.

Marco just stood there, building up adrenaline and patiently waiting, until everyone heard the sound of a loud engine roaring from down the street and then Kenny's piece of junk Woody pulling in through the entry gates of the factory.

No one could believe it, but Kenny was actually showing up for his own funeral!

The car raced in, and skidded sideways to a screeching halt, right next to Marco.

We could see Kenny and Kelly sitting in the front seats, with big clown-like smiles across their faces.

Kenny didn't seem at all concerned that his life would soon be over.

They opened their creaking doors, and Marco began to move forward to destroy Kenny.

When two large men who were hiding in the back seat of Kenny's car emerged!

It was my neighbor Mr. Bundy and Kenny's father!

The two men slowly approached Marco, who was stoically standing his ground.

"Mr. Bundy, so nice to see ya. Please give my regards to your beautiful wife. Tell her I look forward to doing her again," Marco smirked.

"You are dead, you little grease ball," Mr. Bundy replied.

"If I were you, I would leave now before I kill you guys," Marco coolly stated.

"Hey Mr. Johnson, I'm surprised to see you on your feet, aren't you usually drunk and pissing in your pants by this time of the day," snickered Marco.

The two enraged men raced over, and took hold of Marco as Kenny put on his brass knuckles that he had removed from his back pocket.

Then he smugly approached Marco as Kelly sauntered confidently alongside him.

"Did you really think I would show up here alone, Ginzo?" chuckled Kenny confidently.

Kelly marched right up to Marco's face and spit on him. She then proceeded to wildly slap, punch and kick him as he was held in place by the two men.

Her long brown hair was flailing all over the place, and I didn't think she could even see what she was doing.

The crowd was screaming and shouting wildly!

Marco struggled to get away but the men were very large and extremely strong. I feared for him and I didn't know what to do! I had to help him!

I started to run towards them, and I pushed Kelly to the ground!

Kenny grabbed my shirt and prepared to punch me in the face with his brass knuckles.

Then, suddenly the crowd became silent as Kenny zeroed in on my face.

He paused for a moment, as he pulled his fist back, when he suddenly noticed the crowd's attention was turning toward a large black Limo that was slowly entering into the cement factory parking lot.

The car slowly crept up next to Kenny's car and came to a slow then complete halt.

All four doors opened in unison, and four men wearing black gangster coats and dark brimmed hats exited the car, leaving the doors wide open.

"Holy Shit!! It's Marco's father!" I exclaimed.

Kenny dropped his hands, and became pale and limp again. Two of the men grabbed Kenny, and the other grabbed a handful of the back of Kelly's hair and held her against his fist.

Mr. D approached Mr. Bundy and Mr. Johnson as if he had better things to do.

The two men became visibly frightened when they realized who was standing before them.

The Mafia Kingpin of Bakersfield.

"Youz guys seem a little bit too old to be messing with my little boy here. Don't ju think youz should pick on somebody your own size?" sneered Mr. Delgato.

The two men loosened their grip on Marco and looked as if they had just seen a ghost.

"Now, I don't think we are gonna have any more of dat. Let go of my boy," Mr. Delgato calmly ordered.

They quickly released him as Kenny horrifically watched.

"Kick his ass Dad!!" Kenny shouted.

"Yeah...come on, kick my ass Dad," Mr. Delgato mocked.

"Shut up you moron!" shouted Mr. Johnson to Kenny.

For an instant, it seemed that Mr. Johnson was going to attempt a "Hail Mary" swing at Mr. D, but Mr. Delgato quickly punched him in the face with his iron fist before he had the chance.

He hit him in the face so hard Mr. Johnson's false teeth went flying across the parking lot.

As Mr. Johnson hit the ground, Mr. D then turned his attention toward Mr. Bundy who was nervously pulling out a large folding knife from his back pocket. Mr. Delgato grabbed his wrist and effortlessly took the knife away and then stuck it into Bundy's shoulder!

The huge crowd of kids were going wild and Mr. Delgato seemed to be enjoying the energy and the attention.

With much fanfare Mr. D carried on as if he was a prize fighter entertaining his blood thirsty audience!

He then raised his hands provoking the crowd to make a lot of noise as he began beating the living daylights out of big fat Mr. Bundy!

When Mr. Bundy finally blacked out and went down for the count, Mr. Johnson staggered up to his feet, and tried to regain some dignity and took a drunken swing at Mr. Delgato.

Instead he was pummeled in the face over and over again, like a punching bag by Mr. Delgato's raging fists.

He quickly went down once again, and when his head hit the asphalt, it sounded like a watermelon being dropped off a bridge and smashing onto the pavement! There was blood everywhere!

Mr. D's henchmen then pushed Kenny and Kelly to the center of the lot, and then dragged Mr. Johnson and Mr. Bundy's bloody bodies, over to the rear end of the limo.

They spread a plastic sheet over the trunk floor to protect it from their blood, as not to leave any blood evidence behind in the trunks carpeting.

Then they proceeded to hoist up the two men, and they dumped their bodies recklessly into the trunk of the limo and slammed it closed.

The four men then returned back into their car, closed the doors in unison and began to drive off.

The rear window began to roll down and Mr. Delgato stuck his head out and shouted to Marco...

"Hey, it's spaghetti and meatballs night...don't be late for supper!" and they sped off.

Kenny, overwhelmed with fear, then dropped to his knees begging for mercy.

"It was all her fault! She made me beat up Lord because she wanted the drugs!" Kenny pleaded.

"Shut up you stupid ass! You wanted the dope too!" Kelly shouted at him.

Marco ablaze with anger, slowly approached Kenny who was down on his knees already mentally defeated.

He took hold of his greasy blond hair, and gazed up at the crowd.

The sadistic kids were going wild!

It was just as if Marco was a gladiator in the great Roman coliseum, with his heel on the throat of his adversary!

Marco held up his fist to the crowd, and gave them a "thumbs up or thumbs down sign!"

The crowd of blood thirsty kids went crazy!

"Thumbs down! Thumbs down!" they madly shouted and everyone had their thumbs turned down.

Marco gazed down at Kenny who was now crying and whimpering for his life.

"I guess you're going to have to die, you piece of shit!" exclaimed Marco.

Kelly tried to push Marco, so Kenny might have a chance to get away, but Marco quickly grabbed her hair, and twisted it around his hand and he flung her violently down to the ground!

He had a handful of her beautiful hair still clenched in his fist as it tore away from her scalp!

She rolled across the pavement several times, and when she got up and realized Marco ripped her hair right out of her head, she shrieked and put her hand over her bleeding scalp, and ran off through the crowd.

Marco then grabbed a fist full of Kenny's long blond hair and lifted Kenny up to his feet.

Kenny was about a foot taller, and three years older than Marco.

It was odd to see such a mismatch, but everyone knew how brutal Marco could be.

He finally unloaded and hit Kenny with a solid punch to the eye which dazed Kenny.

The crowd went wild and they were shouting "KENNY IS A DEAD MAN!" over and over again!

Marco then followed up by going nuclear and punching him in the side of the head, crushing his cheek bone and then gave Kenny a hard knee kick to his stomach.

I think he was trying to send Kenny's teeth through the side of his mouth, as he had claimed to have done to some other kid years before!

Kenny collapsed to the ground, pretending to be unconscious.

"Oh, you're not getting off that easy!" exclaimed Marco.

He picked up Kenny's limp body, and lifted him completely over his head! Something he always talked about doing after we watched a professional wrestler do that move on TV.

Then he slammed him down on the windshield of his car, smashing a circular indentation into the crushed glass! Kenny rolled off the hood of his car, still wearing his brass knuckles.

Finally Kenny came to life and charged at Marco. I suppose he contemplated that he was already going to the hospital, so why not make the most of it.

He tackled Marco, and brought him down to the ground! He was momentarily on top of Marco and managed to strike Marco on the neck with his brass knuckles but

Marco quickly rolled him over, and was now on top of him.

Marco began insanely pummeling Kenny's face, over and over until Kenny was finally unconscious.

Marco then slowly stood up, and pointed his bloody finger at Kenny's disfigured bloody face.

"Don't you ever mess with my best friend again!" he roared.

Then, Marco noticed an old cement block laying on the ground. He picked it up, and heaved it up over his head. Everyone thought he was going to drop it on Kenny's face! It was sheer pandemonium!

The kids were shouting wildly "Thumbs down! Thumbs down!" for Marco to finish him off. I didn't want this moment to ruin his life, so I ran over to him!

"No Marco...don't kill him! He's not worth going to jail for murder!" I shouted.

Marco momentarily stopped and turned his intention toward me, and then coyly smiled.

Instead of smashing Kenny's head open with the cement block, he dropped it right on Kenny's knee!

Kenny's limp body buckled from the impact and Kenny came back to life, grabbing his knee, and screaming from the excruciating pain!

He began rolling around on the pavement, until he found his way under his car, and hid there.

From the distance, a siren could be heard, and the screaming blood thirsty kids took off back toward the school.

I walked over to Marco and hugged him.

"You are one tough Pizano!" I shouted.

"That piece of shit will never bother you again," Marco stated.

"Come on...let's get out of here before the cops get here!" I exclaimed.

We trotted off, disappearing into the hectic herd of crazed kids.

Within a few minutes the cement factory lot was cleared, and all that remained was Kenny struggling to get out from under his car.

We took a shortcut and walked back to my house, and I asked him if he was scared.

"Scared? I don't know what scared feels like...I only knew that piece of shit needed a severe beating, and I knew if he did show up, he wouldn't have the guts to come alone. I asked my dad to swing by just in case," Marco replied.

"What is going to happen to Mr. Johnson and Mr. Bundy?" I asked.

"They'll most likely have some fun with them, and probably take them up into the mountains and let them believe they were going to get knocked off, before they let them run away. They probably shot at them a few times to really put a scare into them!" Marco chuckled.

When we arrived back at my house, we noticed Mr. Bundy's yard seemed awfully quiet.

Chomper was just laying in his dirt spot, and he struggled to get up when he saw us, but quickly decided it was easier just to stay put and sleep.

My mother saw us coming into the house, and became concerned.

"What in Hell's Bell's happened to you!" she exclaimed.

"Kenny Johnson," I replied.

"Don't worry Mrs. Lord, I gave him the beating of his life. He won't be bothering Donny anymore," gloated Marco.

"Come in boys, let me put some ice on your face Donny, and I think you can use some ice on your hands Marco," my mother stated.

"No thanks, Mrs. Lord. My father told me to be home early for supper, so I better get going," replied Marco.

Marco quickly left out the back door, and I noticed Mr. Bundy scurrying out of the woods into his yard, wearing only his underpants and his bloody tee shirt!

Chomper was just laying there, and barely had the ambition to lift his head and look at his master.

When I returned to the kitchen, my mother informed me that she had some news.

My father's lawyer had called, and stated there might be a slight chance that he might get a commuted sentence. Since it was a nonviolent crime, and because of my dad's record of good behavior in prison.

That was great news, since he had only served two years out of his ten year jail term.

So much time has already gone by though.

Such a waste of life.

Rotting away behind bars, and getting out only after the best years of your life are gone and behind you.

I hope they let him out. It would be good to have him home again.

The phone rang, breaking the silence, and to our surprise, it was my father!

One day a week they allow designated prisoners with good behavior to make a phone call home.

"We were just talking about you, Dad!" I exclaimed. I told him all about the fight, and he was impressed that Marco had the chutzpah to charge into my school and call out Kenny.

"You know son, in prison you have to fight your own battles," he stated.

Reminding me that someday I'll have to take care of my own problems.

I handed the phone to my mother, and went upstairs to do my homework.

I couldn't get that fight out of my mind, and I wondered what might be going on at Kenny's house that evening.

Father and son completely demoralized and obliterated.

It must have made for some comical dinner conversation.

"Gee dad we really got the shit beat out of us today! Can you pass me the mashed potatoes, I can't chew with my broken jaw wired shut?" laughed Kenny.

"I can't chew either son, since my fake teeth got knocked out, and skidded across the parking lot at the cement factory!" chuckled Mr. Johnson.

"Yep, we sure did get a beating today. But I think I'm going to miss seeing those stars that have been swirling around my head all afternoon!" Kenny hysterically laughed .

"Here you go son, you can have my pudding too! I'm still a little car sick from bouncing around in the trunk of that black limo for three hours while Bundy was bleeding all over me!" roared Mr. Johnson as he fell on the floor laughing.

"Dad, do we still have Granny's walker...I think I might need it for a while since my knee is now sawdust!" Kenny's eyes were full of tears as they couldn't stop laughing!

I sat there daydreaming until I heard my mother call me down for dinner.

Chapter 19

My mom was constantly experimenting with new and unusual dinner ideas.

Tonight she informed me we were having a new concoction that she had seen advertised on television.

It was called "Hamburger D'Lux".

All you had to do was dump a hunk of raw hamburger in a frying pan and fry all the grease and grizzle out of it.

Then you add a cup of water to the meat in the pan, and add the included large packet of a mysterious carcinogenic orange powder which is blended with crispy raw pasta and exotic spices.

Next you let it simmer in the greasy watery hamburger gruel for about 20 minutes and Shazam! Dinner is served. My mom slopped a pile of the bubbling ooze on a plate, and slid it across the table in front of me.

"What is this crap?" I asked.

"Hamburger D'Lux...it's the newest thing on TV!

It was either this, or Shake n' bake," my mother stated.

"Mom, are you trying to kill me?" I sarcastically questioned.

"Just try it...it looked good on TV?" she replied.

I hesitantly picked up my fork, and heaved up a generous portion of the sludgy, radioactive bright orange pasta goop.

I didn't have to twirl it or balance it on my fork, because it just adhered itself to it, just like contact cement!

"See it will stick to your ribs!" my mother joked.

I scientifically analyzed the substance which was bubbling like lava on my fork.

First I inhaled it's fumes, in the way I would smell any noxious material.

As I held my fork in my right hand, I waffled the air above the orange "goo" toward my nose with my left hand.

"Hmm, it smells a little bit like pizza," I thought.

I slowly raised the fork to my mouth, and prayed to God that this wasn't going to kill me.

Cautiously, I nibbled on the food sample in the same manner as I had done with the Scungilli.

"Hmmm, not bad," I stated.

Then I vigorously tore into the balance of the bubbling blob on my plate! I even had two more large helpings as my mother was in glee over her cooking success.

"Tomorrow let's have Shake n' Bake!!" I exclaimed.

After supper I went up to my room and worked on some homework.

Oddly, after about a half hour I noticed I was getting really thirsty.

"Gee, that Hamburger D'Lux must have been a little salty," I thought.

I decided that I had better get a drink and I walked down stairs to get a glass of water.

Suddenly I felt a sharp cramping pain come over me, and I felt my gut start to ache and churn!

I could feel gas pressure building up as I reached the bottom of the stairs, and I could hear that my mother was in the kitchen talking on the phone with someone.

There was nuclear Armageddon going on inside of me, and my stomach was angry and generating a massive amount of pressure!

As I entered the kitchen, my gut was ready to explode!

I couldn't hold it in anymore!

I suddenly unleashed the most enormous burst of flatulent gas ever heard by mankind!

In fact, it was so loud my mother had a horrific look on her face, and her conversation abruptly stalled!

I could even hear the woman on the other end of the phone say:

"Are you Okay?!! I heard an explosion!!...Did something blow up?!! Should I call the fire department!" she exclaimed.

"Oh, no, don't worry, that was just Donny farting," my mother replied.

"Who is that you are talking to?!!!" I hysterically whispered.

"Don't worry it's only Judy…Kelly Mosely's mom," she replied.

My face became blood red with embarrassment, and I started to break out into a heated Hamburger D'lux drenching sweat!

Perspiration began pouring over my face as the Niagara River flowed over its falls, and my clothes became soaked with sweat!

"NO, NO, NO! Why are you talking to Kelly Mosely's mother!!? And WHY did you tell her I just farted??!!!" I hysterically whispered again.

My mother looked at me, and shrugged her shoulders and smiled, not realizing the magnitude of the embarrassment and humiliation she had just bestowed upon me!

I gave her the death stare with my eyes bulging out of my head, and then she understood what she had done!

She held up her finger, and whispered,

"Don't worry, I'll fix it," as she continued talking to Kelly's mother.

"So Judy, I just want to explain why Donny farted so loudly…I just bought this new Hamburger D'lux, and I made it for Donny tonight…I guess it made him a little gassy," and she smiled and gave me a big thumbs up! Alas, my short life is now over!

"WHY ARE YOU TALKING TO HER!!" I exclaimed in an extremely desperate whisper.

"She wanted to know what happened at school today. You know, about the fight. She thought I might know something so she called," she whispered back to me as she held her hand over the phone.

I dropped my chin, and shook my head from side to side in disbelief, as I left the kitchen with my glass of water and my tail between my legs and returned to my room.

I just laid there on my bed, humiliated and thirsty.

Tragically, I just stayed in my room and continued passing gas for the rest of the evening.

Chapter 20

The following morning I was supposed to wake up feeling great.

I was confident that I would be able to go to school without being bothered by Kenny anymore.

But now I was weighing the odds and "what if's" if Mrs. Mosely blabbed to Kelly that I farted so thunderously that she thought our house exploded!

Hopefully she just forgot about it, and I'm making a bigger deal about it than it really was.

"Ya, I'm probably just over thinking this," I thought.

I eagerly waited at the end of my driveway for the bus, anticipating all the excitement and chatter that would be going on in the bus and at school today.

All the kids will be talking about the fight, and maybe after this, Kelly and Kenny probably broke up.

Could I forgive her for treating me like dirt? Kicking me in the stomach, and coercing Kenny to beat me up every day for drugs?

"No way! Absolutely not!...Well, possibly, but only if she apologizes and pleads insanity," I reckoned.

The bus screeched to a hard stop in front of me and I hesitantly got on, expecting the door to close on my face, but this time it didn't.

"What's the matter Dwaine, no dumb tricks today?" I asked.

"I don't want you to sick that wacko Marco on me, so I promise to be good from now on," he apologetically stated.

"Hmmm, things are actually looking up for me," I thought as I entered the bus and began walking down the long aisle searching for an empty seat, with dignity and a newly acquired respect. Dwaine suddenly floored the accelerator, and slammed on the brakes!

The momentum threw me back and forth, and I fell down onto the filthy, sticky bus floor!

"Sucker!" he sarcastically shouted back at me, and all the kids once again began laughing at me.

Embarrassed, I struggled to get up from in between the narrow aisle, as he continued accelerating and slamming on the brakes, tossing me about, until I noticed Crystal sitting all alone.

I recklessly managed to get up and I quickly threw myself down next to her.

"So I heard Kenny finally got his due," she quietly stated.

"Oh, you weren't there?" I replied.

"No, I don't like to see that sort of thing," she replied.

I nodded my head, and I understood.

"Donny, I was wondering if you would like to study together sometimes? I could use a little help with chemistry, and I know you are the smartest kid in the school," Crystal hopefully asked.

"Sure Crystal, anytime," I reluctantly replied.

She smiled, and nudged a little closer to me.

I became a bit flustered because I didn't want her to get the wrong idea about "studying together".

Despite everything Kelly had put me through, ridiculously I was still in love with her.

Am I a glutton for punishment?

Probably, but I can't shake the feelings I had for her that day at the waterfall, and maybe if Kenny was out of the picture, things might be different.

"I think maybe Kelly broke up with Kenny!" I blurted out.

Crystal instantly went limp and shifted away from me, and her face instantly lost its glow.

"Who cares! Did you forget how badly she treated you?!" she exclaimed.

I didn't respond, and just sat there staring down at the floor.

The bus screeched to a stop in front of the school and the folding door opened.

"Have a bad day shit heads!" Dwaine shouted.

It felt great not to have to worry about Kenny anymore. But I secretly wondered if things could ever work out between Kelly and me, now that Kenny might be out of the picture.

I stepped off the bus, and took in a breath of fresh air as the sun was rising over the school.

I was now finally free from Kenny's bullying, and I entered the school building as a new man!

I will no longer be the nerd that gets picked on or stuffed into a locker.

I am now an equal citizen of the school's community, and not a punching bag anymore.

As I strolled down the hallway to my homeroom, I noticed some of my science club colleagues excitedly fawning over a poster on the school's bulletin board.

It was a posting for the Spring Science Fair that was designated to be held the last week of school, and the awards and prizes will be awarded on the final day of classes at an all school assembly.

"Things are really looking up!" I thought as I read over the signup sheet.

I'm rid of Kenny, and now the science fair is on!

Life is great! I'm sure to win the grand prize of that pizza dinner for two.

Maybe I'll take Kelly to share in my victory.

I jotted my name on the signup sheet, much to the dismay of my fellow science clubbers.

As I turned around, I was taken aback to see Kelly Mosely leaning up against a locker about ten feet away from me. She was chatting it up with one of her sleazy hippie girl friends, and she was wearing an oversized floppy hat.

Most likely to conceal that big hunk of her scalp that Marco had torn off.

"Maybe she didn't see me," I prayed.

I discreetly turned and ducked off in the opposite direction as I bumped into what seemed to be the entire school population passing through the hallway.

That's when I heard a girl's voice shout up from behind me.

"Hey Donny Lord! ARE YOU STILL SETTING OFF THOSE ATOMIC FARTS FROM THAT HAMBURGER D'LUX YOU ATE LAST NIGHT!" Kelly roared.

It was so embarrassing!! I just wanted to kill my mother!

Everyone in the hallway paused, and it seemed as if the entire school was pointing and laughing at me!

I frantically rushed away through the hallway pushing my way through the gauntlet of humiliation to get to my home room, as I had to endure miles of "Farting noises" and hysterical laughter from all the kids all the way there!

To my dismay, for the rest of the year, the kids kept referring to me as "Fart Boy D'lux".

Just when I thought things were looking up for me, they came flagellating down again.

Chapter 21

The Science fair was on my mind, and I had to decide what I was going to submit.

There was no way I could enter my explosive cherry bombs or mortar rockets, but I thought about the muscle building/aging serum that I injected into Chomper a few months back.

If I can isolate and remove the aging aspect of the serum, maybe I can turn a baby rat into a full grown adult rat in the matter of a few hours? That would be interesting.

I rummaged through my old notes, and found the recipe for the body building serum.

I studied it, and revisited the many chains of chemical configurations.

After a few days and nights, I discovered that by isolating certain DNA proteins, and adding a bit of certain growth hormones, I might be able to cause rapid growth, and eliminate the aging element of the serum.

I immediately began working on the formula and injected a sample of the serum into some mouse cell tissue that I was keeping alive in my refrigerator.

Things were looking promising, and I was able to grow vast amounts of mouse tissue which grew faster using my formula. The only drawback was that the tissue swelled up several hours later and burst, after it quickly multiplied.

I decided that it was time to try the serum on a living creature.

Crud had passed away a few weeks after we initially injected him with the LSD, and since Crud was gone I needed more rats to experiment with.

I asked my mother to drive me to the pet store, and I bought two large rats.

One was a black male, and the other was a white female. In a short time I began breeding the rats for my experiments using the pink bald babies as test specimens.

After tweaking my formula, I was able to speed the growth rate of a newborn baby rat to an adult in just one day! Unfortunately, the rat would be fine until day five. The problem was that on the 5th day the rat would bloat up and die. That was a problem.

The science fair was approaching and I had no time to resolve the issue.

If I timed it properly, I might be able to pull this off. The science fair ran Monday through Thursday and the awards are given out on Friday...I'm hoping the rat will make it through Friday when they crown the victor.

Chapter 22

The school year flew by and the science fair finally arrived. I had set up a table with two cages. There was a baby rat contained in each cage, however one baby was injected with the growth serum and the other was not.

My Science teacher Mr. Casale casually strolled by, and asked me about my experiment.

I told him I could exceptionally facilitate an infant rat's growth rate, from a baby to an adult in just a matter of hours.

"Hmmm, sounds like they may need "Geritol" when they mature!" he joked.

Geritol? I've seen that advertised on TV sometimes. It's some sort of magical liquid vitamin elixir for old people. It's supposed to make old people feel rejuvenated and young again.

When I arrived home that day, I asked my mother if we had any Geritol?

She looked at me in a funny way, and said that she was too young for that, but that she had seen it in the drug store.

I begged her to take me there, and so I bought a small bottle of Geritol for three dollars.

The following morning at school, I injected a few drops of Geritol into the baby rat specimen which had already received the serum injection. Day by day the rat began growing at an alarming rate.

Not only did it mature quickly, but it was growing beyond its normal capacity. I was concerned that it might just die before the end of the week from obesity, and ruin my chances of a win, and owning that Pizza dinner with Kelly.

Whatever was in that Geritol, it was messing with my experiment!

The last day of school finally arrived and it was the grand finale of the science fair.

The Principal arranged an all school assembly in the gym to announce the winner of the science fair at the end of the day.

I was one of the top 3 finalists.

It was between Bruce Slater, a kid in my science club, surprisingly Crystal and me.

Bruce had entered an electric motor that he made out of tinker toys and a dry cell battery connected to a nail.

"I had made one of those in the first grade...so lame," I thought.

Crystal entered a "wind energy" prototype.

It consisted of a pinwheel connected by a rubber band to a small slot car racing motor, which was then connected to a small flashlight bulb.

She used a tiny fan to blow air through the pinwheel, which turned the arbor on the tiny motor, which generated electricity that lit the bulb.

"That was never going to win. Why would anyone use wind to create electricity in this day and age! Oil is so damn cheap! Windmills went out of style back in the 1800's. I have this one in the bag!" I thought as I manically chuckled to myself and rubbed my hands together.

"I'm havin' Pizza tonight... with Kelly!" I proclaimed.

Chapter 23

The Gym was packed to the hilt with students, teachers and administrators.

I gazed up at the large noisy crowd, and noticed a mysterious man wearing dark sunglasses and a very expensive suit. He was watching me from an inconspicuous spot in the corner of the gym.

He actually resembled a Secret Service agent who might be spying on me.

My attention was directed back toward the principal, when he started to clap his hands for silence.

I was becoming a little nervous about my acceptance speech, and very concerned that some idiot might shout out "Fart Boy D'lux" or make vulgar impressions during it.

The principal, Mr. Shultz approached the podium, as the three of us sat in metal folding chairs on the wooden parquet gym floor behind him. Our entries were placed on a table in front of Mr. Schultz, as he spoke from the podium facing the crowd.

"Students, faculty and guests. I would like to congratulate these three finalists of this year's Science fair.

All three of you should be very proud of your work.

It was a very close competition, but unfortunately, there can only be one winner," the principal stated.

As I was sitting there, Crystal leaned over to me, and whispered "Good luck Donny".

I thanked her, and reciprocated back to her "Good luck to you too".

I felt a little bad for Crystal, since I knew she didn't have a prayer of winning.

The principal moved next to the entries, and prepared to announce the winner.

"And the third place finalist is…Bruce Slater's tinker toy electric motor!"

There were a few kids that were half heartedly clapping, and Bruce stood up and shook hands with the principal, and accepted his third place ribbon.

"Here we go!" as I braced myself for the win.

"Second place goes to…" paused Mr. Shultz.

He was leaning toward Crystal's Wind Machine!!

"I'm going to win this!" I silently exclaimed.

Then, suddenly there was a horrible loud shriek and a tumult transpiring from my rat cage exhibit.

Mr. Shultz quickly backed away a safe distance from the table!

Everyone's attention in the gym turned towards my rat cage exhibit, and the fact that my rat was swelling up like a balloon!

It was frantically scampering around the cage, flipping over and over, then freakishly it began inflating and floating to the top of his cage!!

It was now swelling and rapidly expanding to about the size of a basketball! The cage finally couldn't contain it anymore, and it burst apart! The rat was released as he continued floating and expanding in size!

Amazingly the rat slowly began to rise, and float upward! The crowd was stunned as everyone was focused on the enormous rising rat! No one had ever seen a hairy rat turning into a floating hot air balloon before!

The principal awkwardly grabbed its tail, as if it were a string on a balloon, and kept it from floating to the ceiling of the gym!

But, it still continued to expand! Inflating larger and larger!

It was now about the size of a large watermelon, and still growing! The crowd grew silent in amazement as no one could believe what they were seeing!

"That rat couldn't possibly get any bigger? Could it?!" whispered Crystal.

The rat continued expanding, and was now up to the size of a large beach ball, and then suddenly!

A LOUD BANG!!

My rat exploded!!!

Pieces of its body parts splattered everywhere!

Everyone ran screaming and running in all directions, trying to escape the gym! Principal Shultz glared at me, and through the commotion he presented the First Place trophy to… Crystal.

"Man that was bad timing," I thought.

Crystal accepted her prize, and thanked everyone for her victory, even though no one was listening as they were storming out of the gym.

When it was over, the principal angrily approached me.

"What the hell happened, Lord!!" he exclaimed.

"I think that maybe the rat blew up because of the Geritol I injected into him," I replied.

His face became red and angry,

"Ya think Einstein?!" he shouted.

"Clean up this mess, and by the way you are expelled from any future science fairs!" he exclaimed.

He then handed me the rat tail he was still holding onto.

I found a waste can and carefully began picking up the fragmented remains of poor Ratty.

I found his head tangled up in one of the basketball nets, while most of the floor was splattered with tiny bits of hair, mangled tissue and mouse extremities.

I heard a girl scream from down the hallway and apparently she had found his butt end, which had landed in her open purse.

Eeesh,…that was bad luck.

I finally had things mostly cleaned up before the janitor finally arrived and I discreetly left the Gym.

It was time to go home and when I got onto the bus, Dwain was sitting there, passed out with a half empty whiskey bottle in his hand.

Everyone was excited since it was the last day of school and the final ride home for the year.

I noticed Crystal was beaming in the back seat and proudly touting her first place trophy. I miserably sat down in the front by myself, and endured the heckling of each kid who entered the bus.

Crystal moved up behind me and tapped me on the shoulder.

"Hey…I really think you should have won," she softly stated.

And she passed the trophy, and the certificate for the pizza dinner toward me.

"Thanks Crystal, but I literally 'blew it'," I chuckled.

She laughed and it sort of softened things up for me.

Just then I glanced out the bus window, and saw Kenny limping out of his junky Ford Woody wagon, and gimped over towards a large group of the "R.A.F.T." kids that were hanging around the parking lot.

The Rafties, what we referred to them as, were the degenerate boys and girls who rather than drop out, were allowed to enter the program and "go" to school, while basically goofing off and doing next to nothing and still get a diploma.

Otherwise, they had no chance of ever graduating from high school. They had a ridiculously easy curriculum of, "just show up to school and you will pass" to get them through high school.

No one really knew what R.A.F.T. stood for, but we had a lot of fun coming up with our own acronyms for it.

The motley group that Kenny was heading toward was composed of the teenagers who were big trouble makers, bullies, pot smokers, glue sniffers, sluts and teenage drunks. Kenny fit right in with that bunch.

I watched him as he approached the crowd and he reached into his tee shirt pocket fumbling to pull out a fresh pack of Marlboros.

He began rapidly hitting the closed pack against the palm of his hand to set the tobacco, then he opened it and began passing out cigarettes to the kids.

When he turned to leave, I noticed him playfully pulling a girls arm out from the large group.

It was Kelly Mosely.

She jumped on his back, and forced him to carry her back to his car, as he limped on his lame leg. She was laughing, and kicking him as if he was a horse.

Too bad for Kenny, it seemed that his leg would never be right after what Marco had done to it.

When they finally reached his car, she hopped off him and she jumped into the passenger seat. Kenny scurried around to the driver's side, and eagerly fell into his car.

He started his car, and raced the toasted engine until it began backfiring. Then he went on to grind up the gears a bit, and when he finally jammed the car into gear, he burned his tires out of the school parking lot, laying a strip of rubber all the way down the street.

Crystal watched me as I was in a daze, watching Kelly leave with Kenny.

"I guess Kenny and Kelly haven't been bothering you for drugs since your friend beat them up," she stated.

There was a pause of silence, as I digested the fact that Kelly was still with that loser, Kenny.

"Yeah," I dismally replied.

Crystal tapped me on the back of my shoulder with the trophy.

"Hey, I have an idea! Why don't we share the Pizza prize and go together?!" she exclaimed.

I watched the smoke clear from Kenny's burnout, and saw my dream girl go up in smoke with it.

I turned to Crystal,

"I think that's a great idea, we should do that," I happily stated.

The bus rumbled out of the parking lot, and we made our plans to meet for Pizza that night.

"Did you get your report card today?" she inquired.

"Yes, all A+'s except for Art and Gym," I replied. Crystal paused waiting for me to ask her about her report card.

"Um, how did you do?" I asked.

"Well, I got mostly A's and B's except for a "C+" in chemistry," she regretfully stated.

Ouch! That was a big dig, because she had asked me for help with her chemistry several months ago, and I never did get around to help her. I quickly changed the subject:

"So what kind of pizza do you like?"

"Definitely Pepperoni!" she replied.

"Alright, since you won the prize, you get to choose!" I joked.

The bus stopped in front of my house and I heard the bus door swing open. I told Crystal I would meet her at

five o'clock at the pizza house.

"See you later, Windmiller-ator" I joked.

Just then someone shouted from the back of the bus…

"Get off the bus! Lord Fart D'Lux!".

I turned beet red and I rushed to get off the bus.

Dwain sluggishly closed the door in front of me, and I crashed into it as I rushed to exit!

"Hey kid!" he slurred.

I thought he was going to say something profound since it was the end of the year...maybe an apology for all the rotten things he had done to me. But instead he said:

"I'm sooo drunk…Ass wipe!" and he threw me the finger as he opened the door again, and he pushed me out with his foot.

I fell down the steps, and he quickly closed the door behind me and pulled away as I laid there on the street.

I looked up and saw Crystal excitedly waving to me, and holding up five fingers.

Chapter 24

I strolled into my house, and tossed my report card on the kitchen table for my mother to see, and I went upstairs to my room and just laid down on my bed.

No homework, no projects, no more mean kids.

I'm just going to relax for a while before my big date with Crystal.

As I just began to drift off, I was abruptly awakened by the loud rumbling of Mr. Bundy's motorcycle charging up the street.

I jumped up, and looked out my window and I noticed Mrs. Bundy was in the backyard and visibly upset, as she was standing and staring down at a sleeping Chomper.

He was just laying there in the same spot, just as he had been for the past two days.

Mr. Bundy charged into his driveway and quickly dismounted his motorcycle, and ran into the backyard where his wife was. He saw Chomper catatonically lying there, and he fell to the ground and began sobbing.

Chomper was dead!

Apparently, for the past two days to boot.

What a scene, the two of them, who never paid much attention to Chomper in the past, were now blubbering away, now that he was gone. She couldn't stop wailing and finally she had to run back into the house to get a tranquilizer pill.

As soon as she left, Mr. Bundy instantly stopped crying.

He looked around to see if anyone was watching, then ran into the garage for a garbage bag and a shovel.

He quickly began loosening up the top layer of soil near Chomper's dog house, and threw several shovelfuls of dirt from his garden on top of it, and made it look as if he had dug a small rectangular grave and buried Chomper.

Then he shoved Chompers stiff carcass into a plastic garbage bag, and quickly stuffed it into their garbage can!!

Mrs. Bundy had returned from the house shortly after, and placed a rose on the dirt mound where she believed Mr. Bundy had buried Chomper. Mr. Bundy even voiced some sort of half-assed eulogy and prayer for Chomper, and then they ridiculously sang Amazing Grace together!

Mrs. Bundy couldn't control her emotions as she was hysterically crying the entire time.

Finally, they both turned arm in arm and slowly went inside.

I felt a little sorry for Chomper, though.

I knew I was responsible for him aging, and he probably had a few more years of killing left in him. But if the police would have captured him after he killed that bull, and tore the dog warden's arm off, he would have been euthanized many years ago.

I suddenly heard the porch door slam, and my mother walked into the house with the mail.

"Yay! The last day of school!" she shouted.

I hurried down the stairs and I found her standing in our kitchen with a man.

It was that secret service guy I had seen at the gym today, during the science fair.

"How was school today, Donny?" she giddily asked.

"Oh no, I hope this guy is not who I think he is!" I cringed.

"Donny, do you know who this man is?" she asked.

"Please Mom! Don't tell me he is going to be my new daddy!!" I exclaimed.

They both burst out laughing!

"No you silly boy...this is Mr. Blackstone. He is our state Senator, you silly boy!" she laughed.

"Hmm, why was the Senator watching me at school, and now he is at my house?" I thought.

"Donny, I'm sure you are wondering why I am here. The United States government is very interested in you.

Let's go out for dinner tonight and we can discuss it," he suggested.

I felt awkward talking to this strange person, but agreed to go with him, as long as my mother came along too.

Just then I remembered my date with Crystal!

"Uhmm, I'm sorry sir, can we do this another time? I had made plans with a friend to meet up for pizza at five o'clock," I stated.

"Son, this is going to be really important for you and your family.

I drove all the way down from Los Angeles to see you today. How about you call your friend, and push your pizza plans till tomorrow night?" the Senator suggested.

"I know where she lives, but I don't know her number. And her parents are not listed in the phone book," I replied.

"Ohhh, you have a date with a Girl?!" my mother swooned.

I became very embarrassed, and my face turned beet red.

"She's just a friend," I cowardly stated.

"Oh by the way, how did your science fair go, did you win?" she inquired.

I shook my head as I looked at the floor.

"It was a blast," I regretfully replied.

"It sure was, Mrs. Lord! Okay Donny, this is what I can do. Go meet up with your friend, and when you are done we can meet back here, and have that chat," said the Senator.

I gratefully nodded in agreement, and excused myself.

As I marched up the stairs to my room I was puzzled and couldn't help wondering what was going on with the Senator. Why was he really here?

Chapter 25

I was running late, and I quickly rode my bike to the Pizza House.

I arrived just a few minutes past five o'clock.

Crystal was eagerly waiting outside on the sidewalk for me.

"I almost thought you weren't going to show up," she joked.

"I almost didn't! Some Senator guy stopped by my house after school and he wants to talk to me about something. He wanted to take my mom and I out to dinner but I told him I already had plans with you," I replied.

"Oh, I hope it's nothing serious," she asked.

"I think it may have something to do with my dad getting out of prison early," I blurted out.

"Ugh, why did I just say that!" I thought to myself.

I wasn't sure if she knew my dad was in San Quentin, but I would have preferred that she didn't know about it.

If she didn't know before, she knows now.

"Uhh, it's sort of a secret about my dad.

It's a little embarrassing that he is doing time, but it's not like he's a murderer or anything like that," I stated.

Crystal didn't know what to say, so she suggested we go inside, and find a place to sit.

The restaurant was busy, and we found a booth right up front, next to the large picture window facing the street.

"What kind of pizza would you like to order?" she asked.

That broke the awkward route of the conversation, and I smiled.

"Definitely Pepperoni!" I exclaimed.

And she happily agreed.

We ordered the pizza, and sipped our sodas as we sat across from each other, and we joked about the disaster at the science fair that afternoon!

The laughing paused for a moment, and she seemed that she had something on her mind.

"Ya know Donny, my dad is a really successful defense attorney, maybe he could do something to get your father out of jail?" she suggested.

"Thanks, but I don't think there is much that can be done. The IRS is pretty tough on tax evaders," I replied.

"Let me know if you change your mind?" said Crystal.

"By the way, Crystal. If your dad is so successful why aren't you in some fancy shmancy private school?" I inquired.

"My parents were both products of the public school system, and they like the diversity of public vs. private schools," she replied.

"Yeah diversity…Bullies, druggies, sluts, racists and clicks…great reasons to attend public schools," I chuckled.

I was really getting comfortable with Crystal, and I noticed that she was sort of pretty once she let her auburn hair down, took off the orthodontic retaining strap from her mouth and removed her pink "cat eye" glasses.

I was actually enjoying my date with her!

From where we were sitting, We could see and hear the cars and trucks passing by as we waited for our food.

It was a little noisy, but the noise got much worse when I noticed the loud rumbling exhaust of a junk car, as it barreled down the street and made its way in our direction. It finally screeched to a stop down the street a bit from the Pizza House, and my worst fear was realized in that I recognized the sound of that car.

It was Kenny's piece of shit Woody!

"Oh, no!!…That sounds like Kenny's car outside.

Let's hope he isn't coming in here!" I jokingly whispered.

About a minute later, I noticed Kelly walking up the sidewalk, heading our way, and Kenny limping along behind her.

I watched them intently, as they were heading in our direction!

"Pleeeease don't come in here! Please don't come in here!" I prayed.

Kelly then made a bee line directly to the entrance of the restaurant!

The door swung open, and they immediately saw us sitting there next to the front window.

The first thing Kenny did was panic, as he quickly surveyed the restaurant to see if Marco was with us. When he realized that we were alone, he relaxed, and they continued into the restaurant.

They smugly strolled past us, and acted as if we were not even there. It was so awkward, and the tension was filling the room.

They sat down about four tables away, and were whispering back and forth to each other, presumably about us, and laughing as Kelly kept glancing over in our direction.

As I was watching them, Crystal was watching me, watching Kelly.

"So, it's the last day of school. What are your plans for the summer?" Crystal interjected.

"Uh yeah, I never liked anchovies," I replied.

She could see I was obsessively, masochistically absorbed with Kelly, and instantly wasn't paying any attention to her.

Suddenly out of nowhere, I felt a cold harsh slap across my face, shattering my trance-like fixation on Kelly!

"Ya know Donny! I really don't understand you!

That girl over there has treated you like shit from day one! She had you brutally beaten up every day for drugs! She kicked you in the stomach, and she broadcasted to the whole school about you farting up your house, and you still can't get over her!!" shouted Crystal.

She quickly gathered her things, and ran out of the restaurant crying, just as the pizza arrived at our table.

I felt so terrible...but she was right.

I need to put this to an end!

I boldly stood up, and approached the table where Kenny and Kelly were sitting. They were stunned to see me stop right at their table side!

"Kelly can I have a word with you privately?" I asked.

She made a ridiculous face at Kenny, and I could see she was reluctant.

"Please Kelly, it's important," I stated.

She hesitated but then she cautiously stood up, and seemed intrigued about why I wanted to talk to her.

She followed me into the back restroom area, and I turned to face her.

"I'm really confused Kelly. We used to be best friends when we were younger. We rode our bikes and played together almost every day. Our time at the waterfall was the best day of my life and I thought we had something really special between us that day. Something that was incredibly everlasting. I was hoping that when high school started, I thought we could be friends again. Maybe more than friends? I don't understand why you've been acting so mean to me?" I somberly asked.

She was silent as she gazed down at the floor.

"If you don't know, I'm not going to tell you!" she recklessly stated, and she began to turn away to leave.

"Wait, wait don't turn away from me! I DON'T KNOW WHY! I haven't seen you since you started middle school.

It was like you dropped off the face of the Earth! How could I have done anything to you?" I desperately pleaded.

"Really?? Are you that stupid Donny?" she replied.

"Remember that day we were together in the woods? The last day of summer before school started? I had the best day ever with you, when you brought me to your "Secret Waterfall!"

After that day I felt as if we were soul mates destined to be together forever! I realize we were only twelve years old, but I was so in love with you!

I thought you felt the same way about me, then you abandoned me the very next day. I never heard from you again! So many times I would look out my window, and see you riding your bike past my house, and I watched you as you drove away!

If you actually cared about me you would have gotten off your bike, knocked on my door, and taken me in your arms and kissed me! But you never did!

I thought you didn't care about me, so I tried to forget you! I went out and got mixed up with a bad crowd of kids at school, because they made me feel good.

When I saw you again at high school, I wanted to hurt you, the way you hurt me!" she cried.

I couldn't believe what I was hearing!

"That day at the waterfall, lying next to you on the grassy shore after we jumped in the pond. I held your hand and we watched the clouds pass over us, that moment I'll never forget, and I was in love with you too! I wanted to kiss you but I was too scared! I purposely rode by your house hoping you would see me, and that you would come running outside, and grab me and kiss me and tell me that you loved me!" I cried.

We both were standing in front of each other crying, and we slowly moved toward each other and raised our arms to embrace.

But, that's when Kenny showed up, and she caught herself, and abruptly backed away from me.

I didn't even care that Kenny was standing there.

"You are so beautiful, why him?!" I exclaimed.

"Because he asked me and you didn't!" she cried.

Kenny made a goofy face and shrugged his shoulders, and Kelly turned away and quickly walked off. Kenny hustled behind her with his bad limp struggling to keep up with her, and he tried to reach out and put his arm around her shoulders, but she shrugged him off.

Then she suddenly stopped, and turned back to me…

"I'm not the same 'Kelly' you once knew Donny. You should go find Crystal, she's nothing like me. She's a 'Good girl' and I am a 'No good bitch!'" she scowled.

Then she turned away, and marched back to her seat.

Kelly was visibly upset and my heart was crushed.

I felt as if I was that rat that exploded all over the gym that afternoon. My insides were totally blown to pieces!

I left the restaurant out the back door. I don't even know what happened to the pizza.

As I rode my bike home, I couldn't believe how screwed up things had gotten between Kelly and me.

I loved her, she loved me. But for some unknown reason neither of us could figure out how to be together.

We were just two dumb kids at the time, who didn't know any better.

But unfortunately, there is no turning back time and maybe that door just wasn't really meant to be opened.

Chapter 26

As I rode my bike home, I thought about Crystal, and how terribly I messed things up with her too. She must feel as hurt as I do.

But one good thing came out of this day. My mind was clear now. I'm done with Kelly Mosely.

I'll have a talk with Crystal in a few days, after she gets over being angry with me. I'll have all summer to patch things up with her.

I finally made it back to my home, and pedaled into my driveway.

Senator Blackstone's car was still there, and he was inside talking with my mother. As I walked in, I noticed the two of them drinking tea at the kitchen table, and my mother rushed over to greet me.

"How was your date?" asked the Senator.

"Remember what happened at the Science Fair today? Well, the same thing happened to me on my date," I replied.

"Hmm, that's not good, but Donny I do have some very exciting "good" news for you and your family.

A wonderful opportunity awaits you!" stated the Senator.

I was a bit puzzled, and I really didn't understand what he was talking about.

"Did I win some sort of prize or something?" I asked.

The Senator laughed, and opened up his briefcase. He reached in, and retrieved an envelope that was addressed to my father at the San Quentin Prison.

"Do you remember sending this letter to your father last Summer?" the Senator asked.

I took the letter, and I saw it had been opened, and had a large red rubber stamping on it that read: "INTERCEPTED FOR REVIEW: PRISONER MAIL".

I took the letter out, and glanced over it.

"Yeah, I remember this letter. It was about the body building serum that I was messing around with. I'm not in trouble am I?!" I nervously asked.

"No, No you are not in any trouble son. All mail that comes into the prison has to be opened, and inspected by the security guards. Some people try to send in all sorts of inappropriate things, like drugs in the prison mail. They've actually found LSD hidden underneath some of the postage stamps!" the Senator stated.

I awkwardly glanced at my mother, and jumped to my feet.

"I didn't do it! It was her! She did it!" I joked.

"Very funny, Jerry Lewis," she replied.

"Son, a screening guard read this letter, and was impressed enough by it that he sent it up to the warden.

The warden sent it over to the governor, and the governor sent it to me.

You're a pretty smart kid, and the state of California is very impressed with you, son. In fact we are so impressed that I got together with my constituents, and we would like to help you expand your interests in the field of science," he stated.

I was standing next to our kitchen table, and wondering what the hell was so remarkable about that letter. All that I wrote my dad about was that I mixed up some chemicals, and blow darted Chomper in the neck with it. Then he had a bad reaction, and morphed into an old hound dog.

"Sir, with no disrespect. All I did was write about a failed experiment of a fantasy body building serum that I was messing around with, and it was a complete failure.

In fact, it had really bad ramifications.

And after today's results at the science fair, as you witnessed for yourself, I'm not that impressive, in fact I am quite the failure," I sadly stated.

"Son, have you ever heard of WD-40?" asked the Senator.

"Sure that's the spray oil in a can. I have some in the garage," I replied.

"Do you know where that crazy name came from?" he asked.

I just shrugged my shoulders.

"I guessed it just stood for Wet Dog-40," I chuckled.

The Senator laughed.

"WD-40 was invented as a rust inhibitor for the aerospace industry. The WD stands for "Water Displacement". It took three scientists thirty nine failures to get the formula right. On the fortieth try, they were successful.

That's where the name "WD-40" came from. What I'm trying to say is...If every scientist gave up after a failure, we would still be living in the stone age.

How many tries did it take for you to perfect that LSD you were fabricating in your basement?" he asked.

"You know about that?" I said.

"We know everything about you kid! The Cherry bombs, nitroglycerin, fireworks...even those X-ray specs, and the sea monkeys you bought!" he laughed.

"Gee, you guys are pretty good," I replied.

"So here's what we would like to offer you Donny.

As of today you are a high school graduate. Hell, you are a thousand times smarter than any of those idiot teachers in that school. You should have received your diploma years ago," he stated.

"You can do that?" I asked.

"I can do that," he replied.

"Next we are going to arrange for your father to get an early release from prison. We interviewed him extensively about your work, and he was very helpful," stated the Senator.

My mother was overjoyed by that news, but I was still very puzzled.

"Is there anything else?" I suspiciously asked.

"Yes son, there is. You will be receiving a full scholarship to the California Institute of Technology!" he exclaimed.

I suddenly felt as if I had inhaled a helium balloon!

All the air that surrounded me became thin, and I felt as if I was in a dream. My eyes widened and I glanced over at my mother who was just about tearing all her hair out of her head in jubilation!

"I'm going to Caltech!?" I exclaimed.

The Senator smiled and nodded his head.

"Senator Blackstone, with no disrespect, why are you doing this for me? I'm not sure I can even compete with those geniuses at Caltech. I might just flunk out after the first semester," I apprehensively stated.

"Donny, you have been held back by the public school system your whole life. No one seemed to recognize your potential, or went the extra mile for you. We believe that in the right environment, that you are going to change this world.

About a year ago your school required that all the students in your class were to take an IQ test. No one thought much about it, since the kids were told that it didn't matter what grades they got. Do you remember taking that test?" he asked.

"Sure I remember. I finished it in ten minutes," I replied.

"Actually you completed it in seven minutes and forty seven seconds. I have your results right here," stated the Senator.

He reached into an inside jacket pocket, and removed a long white envelope.

"Top Secret" in red ink was stamped on the envelope, and also stamped was the seal of the United States Department of Justice, the Central Intelligence Agency and the Federal Bureau of Investigation! The Senator opened the envelope, and removed two sheets of paper from it.

He put on his glasses, and began reading the letter aloud to us:

Dear Senator Blackstone, After review by the Federal Bureau of investigation and other Investigative agencies of the United States of America we are all unanimous in concluding that Mr. Donald Lord (no middle initial) did not undermine, tamper or cheat on the USA IQ Examination. His score of 191 is one of the highest scores ever recorded by an adolescent boy. Although no test is fool proof we believe this young man is the real deal.

Sincerely,
J. Edgar Hoover

The Senator folded up the paper, and placed it back into the envelope and handed it to me. I didn't know what to say.

My mother was carrying on, bragging to the Senator that she always knew I was a genius, and that her father was once a professor at Berkeley.

"So when do I get to start Caltech?" I smugly asked.

"It's already set up. You will start the summer term in three weeks. You will be placed in special private housing on campus with a chaperone. This will get you used to things before the Fall semester starts," he stated.

"That doesn't give me much of a summer break. When will my dad get out?" I inquired.

"Tomorrow your father will be home.

We didn't want your father being incarcerated to be a distraction to you while at CalTech," he replied.

My mother and I were thrilled that my father would at last be coming home, and it appeared, "Thanks to me!".

"Donny I have to tell you that this is not totally a free ride. The government is investing hundreds of thousands of dollars into you. Whatever you formulate, invent, create, and even your ideas will be the property of the US government.

At some point you will be asked to formulate things, whether they be chemical, molecular or organic, that will align with the needs of the United States government.

It may go against your principles, religious beliefs, or your moral or ethical fabric. Regardless, you will be obligated to perform for your country.

You will also be committed to be employed by your government until you are of the age of 30. Beyond that, you can either continue working for the government, or go off on your own.

However, you and your parents must sign a contract that you agree and will abide by these terms and conditions.

If you break the agreement it can be very bad for you and your father. I just want to make it clear that this unbelievable opportunity for you has strings attached," he sternly looked me in the eyes, and seriously stated.

"What if I don't work out, and maybe I am not as smart as you guys think? Maybe I can't produce what the government wants me to. If they want a cure for cancer, and I can't discover it? Then what?!" I exclaimed.

"As long as you try your best, and we'll know if you aren't, it'll be okay.

We want you to be happy. The happier you are, the more you will produce. Your salary will begin immediately.

The more degrees you earn, the higher your salary will become. For now you will be starting off at $25,000 per year while you are attending undergraduate school.

Also, when you get to Caltech you will be handed the keys to a brand new car. Just let me know what your choice and color are. Do you have your driver's license yet?" he inquired.

"I just turned 16. But, uh no, not yet," I replied.

"Consider it done," and he winked at me.

"I just want this to be crystal clear Donny. Your teenage ass will be the property of the US government for a long time. If you breach your contract there will be major ramifications.

Otherwise you will be a very wealthy young man. So do we have a deal?" the Senator asked, and he reached out with his hand for a handshake.

"Deal!" I exclaimed.

And we vigorously shook hands.

"I'll bring the contract over by the beginning of the week for you and your parents to look over and sign.

You might want to let an attorney look it over, however it's pretty cut and dry. It's been a pleasure meeting you both," he stated.

Then the Senator stood up, put on his jacket and hat, and began walking toward the door.

"Hey Senator Blackstone!" I called out.

He stopped and turned to me.

"A bright red Corvette convertible with white wall tires!" I eagerly stated. He tipped his hat and smiled.

"Nice choice kid, you got it," and he walked out the door.

Chapter 27

Now, for the first time in my life, I felt as if I was worth something besides being a tool for my dad's drug habit. It was a dream, and it felt as if I was one of those high school basketball players that just got recruited by a big time college, with all the perks and amenities.

A full scholarship to an Ivy league school. A load of money, and a new sports car! Take that and stuff it, Principal "Expelled for life from the science fair," Schultz!

My mother instantly got on the phone and began calling all her friends and relatives, bragging about the good news of my scholarship to Caltech, and that my father was soon coming home!

I wandered upstairs, and looked up the California Institute of Technology in my Collier's Encyclopedia. That's how we used to get our information about things before the internet came along.

I was so restless, I couldn't fall asleep for hours. Not so much about Caltech, and my new adventure in life, but about Kelly Mosely. How did our wires get so mixed up?

If only I had the guts, and the fortitude to knock on her door just one day, or a week, or even a month after our time at the waterfall. Everything could have been so different.

Maybe she wouldn't have fallen in with the Northie crowd. I would have been a positive influence on her life, and kept her on a straight path.

I knew we were just kids, and possibly it could have just fizzled out after a few months, but maybe not, we had such a strong connection.

Now, we'll never know. Just as the water rushed over the top of my secret waterfall in the woods, so did my brief moment to be with Kelly Mosely. And for the first time, I really understood the term "Water under the bridge".

Once it flows down the river it's gone forever.

I really felt bad about Crystal too. All she ever wanted was for me to like her. But I was too enamored with Kelly to realize what I had right in front of me, and I should have given her a real chance.

"I need to make things right with Crystal," I decided.

Then I finally fell asleep.

Chapter 28

The following morning, I woke up early and I rode my bike to Crystal's house. It was a huge red brick house with a four car garage set off to the side. One of the garage bays was opened and I noticed a shiny new silver Rolls Royce parked inside!

"Wow, I guess her dad really is successful!" I thought as I passed by the garage.

Their yard was huge, and there was a landscaping service tending to the gardening and mowing of the massive lawn.

I swallowed hard, and built up the courage to walk up the steps to the front door.

I marched up the massive brick staircase, which was guarded by two life sized marble African lion statues. One on each side at the base of the stairs. When I finally reached the top of the steps. I stood before two large, ornately paneled, black lacquer wooden doors. Each was adorned with a large polished brass lion head door knocker.

I nervously lifted one of the brass lion heads and tapped it twice against the door. I waited there for about a minute, and then the door slowly opened. There was an older Hispanic woman wearing a black and white maid's outfit, who was staring at me oddly.

"What ju want?" she rudely stated.

"I am looking for Crystal," I replied in a slow clear voice.

"She not here, go away!" the woman barked, and she slammed the door shut!

I really needed to talk to her, and I was not about to give up that easy! I lifted the door knocker again, and firmly tapped it five times! The woman returned and angrily flung the door open!

"I tol ju, to get da hell out a here!" she shouted.

"I'm not leaving until I see Crystal!" I exclaimed.

Just then a slender, sophisticated woman came out from behind the door, and dismissed the maid. She was an extremely beautiful woman, with the same auburn hair and green eyes as Crystal.

"You must beee, Donny?" the woman sarcastically stated.

"I'm Crystal's mother and I've heard a lot about you Donny. Crystal told me you were a "nice boy" but by the way you treated her yesterday, you don't seem so nice to me. She came home very upset, and you really hurt her feelings. I told her that maybe you are NOT such a nice boy after all and that "The apple doesn't fall far from the tree," now does it Donny?" she sarcastically stated.

I think she was implying that since my father was a convicted felon, that I was a bad seed too.

Maybe I deserved that, for hurting Crystal. So I tried to ignore her derogatory comments.

"Can I just speak to Crystal for a moment?" I pleaded.

"She's not here. She left early this morning for summer camp, and she will be gone all summer at camp so she can forget about you and you should forget about her! She's out of your league!" she rudely stated.

She stepped back, and began to close the door.

"Can you please tell her I stopped by to apologize!" I begged.

"No, I probably won't! Now get lost, you scumbag! And don't ever come back here again!" she sternly stated, then she slammed the door shut.

I remorsefully turned away, and cried as I meandered back to my bike. I sure did mess things up with both girls. For a genius, I have a lot to learn about women.

Chapter 29

I slowly rode my bike home, licking my wounds.

When I finally arrived at my street, I noticed a long black limousine backing out of my driveway. I pedaled as fast as I could, and drove over Mr. Bundy's front lawn, taking the shortest possible route to my front door. I didn't even bother using the kickstand on my bike. I just threw it on the ground, and raced into the house.

My dad was home!!

I heard him laughing in the kitchen, and when I saw him, he jumped up, and we hugged so tightly! He was kissing me over and over!

"I missed you so much, Donny!" he exclaimed.

"I'm so proud of you son! For taking care of your mom, and the house while I was gone".

Mom was preparing a festive lunch, she was so happy to have dad home too.

As he sat down at the table, I thought about how much he had aged. He was only 41 when he went in. And now, after two years of prison, he looked like my grandfather. His hair was now partially gray, and his face was leathery looking with quite a few wrinkles.

"It feels so good to be home!" he exclaimed.

"It feels so good to have you home!" both my mother and I replied.

"What's for lunch!?" I exuberantly asked.

"Since your father has been away, he has been missing out on "Hamburger D'Lux", so I whipped up a batch!" she eagerly replied.

"Seriously Mom!! I can see the headlines….

Husband explodes on his first day home from prison from consuming a toxic mass of Hamburger D'Lux!" I exclaimed.

"Well I don't want to shock his system by going from yucky prison food to fine dining with Chef Boyardee!" she joked.

"Okay what are we really having?" I asked.

"Scungilli!" she joked.

"Really?!!" I exclaimed.

"No...we are having Hamburger D'Lux," my mother laughed.

I gave up and shook my head in disbelief.

"Dad you're not going to believe what I ate at Marco's house! Scungilli!" I exclaimed.

Did Mrs. D make that for you?" he asked.

"Yeah, I didn't think I would like it, but Mr. D forced me to try it. It was so good!" I exclaimed.

My father leaned back in his chair, and tilted his head back, and looked up at the ceiling. He closed his eyes and smiled.

"Yeah, everyone wants a piece of Mrs. D's Scungilli," he swooned.

"Okay dad, you are not in prison anymore, and Mom is looking at you strangely!" I whispered.

I quickly burst his daydream bubble, just as Marco had popped mine in their kitchen. But we gazed at each other with a new kinship, that we both understood. That Mrs. D's Scungilli was amazing!

As we ate our lunch, my father couldn't get over his new found freedom.

"The Warden and some other G men kept asking me a lot of questions about you son. Then one day, the guards were whispering to one another, and eyeballing me. They finally unlocked my cell, and asked me to come with them to see the warden. I thought it was so odd, because they actually asked me instead of just opening the cell door, and dragging me out. They didn't handcuff me or shackle me either. When I arrived at the warden's office, the Warden sat me down and told me he had great news! The Governor issued me "Conditional Probation". I thought I was dreaming until the Warden handed me one of his Cuban, Cohiba cigars, and lit it for me! I went from zero to hero in five minutes!" he exclaimed.

I was like, bewildered. Then it hit me.

"What sort of conditional probation?" I apprehensively asked.

The Warden explained that the government was interested in Donny's scientific aptitude. He said that if Donny takes the college scholarship deal, and works for the government, I am free to go home! I suppose you took the deal?!" rejoiced my father.

"I've been thinking about it. But now that I know that I'm in high demand, maybe I should shop around, and maybe get a better deal from MIT or something?" I joked.

"No!!! If you don't take this deal I will go back to the joint!" my father angrily shouted.

My mother and I were both shocked at my father's sudden harsh outburst. Prison had changed him. The years of confinement and living with hardened criminals had taken its toll on my father.

"Jeezz, I was only kidding!" I exclaimed.

My father regained his composure and apologized.

"Sorry I overreacted...It's hell in that place, and I don't ever intend on going back there. The guards treat you like animals. The animals treat you like garbage. The garbage treats you like shit, and so it goes. Darwin's law…Survival of the fittest.

When I first arrived at San Quentin, I went through the gauntlet of the caged in criminal inmate population. They watched us from the inside of their enclosures, and chanted "Fresh fish! Fresh fish!" over and over as we were prodded along by the guards. I was locked up in a 7'x10' cell with a guy named Stanislov. He was a Russian immigrant who had been living in Sacramento. He was convicted for aggravated assault on a federal employee.

Talk about bad luck. He was married to a woman who made his life miserable. He constantly referred to her as "My Bitch Wife". They fought all the time. He said that he came close a few times wanting to belt her, but he never actually hit her.

One day he came home early from work, and caught his wife with the postman in his bedroom! The naked postman jumped up, pushed Stan down and took off down the stairs and out the front door, dragging his mailbag stuffed with his clothes behind him!

He was high tailing it down the street to his mail truck. When Stan took off down the stairs after him, and realized that he was too far ahead and he wouldn't be able to catch him. He looked down and noticed his son's wooden baseball bat leaning against the porch wall.

He was so full of rage that he picked up that bat, and flung it as hard as he could at the postman.

It twirled through the air, spinning like the rotor of a helicopter! Stan stood there watching as the bat spun wildly through the air. Spinning faster and faster, and accelerating towards its target! Before the postman could get into his truck, that bat came spinning out of the sky, and whacked him across the back of his head! It was a one in a million shot, and even Stan couldn't believe it! Well, a neighbor called the police and Stan was arrested for assaulting a federal agent of the United States Postal Service. It didn't matter that he was having an affair with his wife.

Everyone in prison has a freaky story like that. Some unusual circumstance that landed them in the joint, and each one of them claims to be innocent, of course.

But they all have no choice but to sit and wait out their time. Some go in as teenagers and leave when they are old men. I was lucky to get out while I'm still young enough," my father happily stated.

"Dad, I have a question for you. I know you were severely claustrophobic. How did you manage being handcuffed and locked into that tiny room?" I asked.

My father hesitated, and rubbed his hair back reflecting about it.

"Since I was out on bail until my sentencing, it wasn't a problem for me, although I thought about it sometimes. I really didn't think I was going to do any jail time. My lawyer thought for sure I would get a suspended sentence since no one was really hurt, and I would most likely get off with a hefty fine.

Instead the judge made an example out of me and threw the book at me. When they shackled me after sentencing, I started to freak out in the private hallway behind the courtroom that leads down to the PTV (Prisoner Transport Vehicle). One of the US Marshals that was walking with me saw it coming on and coached me through a deep breathing, relaxation exercise. I started to feel a little better, but when they started to put me in the back of the PTV...I lost it!

I collapsed to the ground and begged them not to put me inside! A Marshal had a special sedative drug ready, and he injected into me as

I was freaking out on the ground, begging them to let me ride up front with them!

About twenty seconds later I was feeling pretty good, and I didn't care what the hell they did with me! They could have strapped me into the electric chair and I would have been asking them for a light bulb!

They hoisted me up, and put me in the back of the PTV as if I was a loaf of bread going into the oven! A few hours later it started to wear off. But my brain was in a better place, I realized I was in no real danger, so I continued breathing deeply which helped.

When the guards brought me to my cell, I suddenly realized how small it was, and that I would be locked in there with no way out! I started to freak out again. Then a guard jabbed me with another tranquilizer shot! I woke up the next morning, and I was better. They gave me a little white pill every day, and before long I was desensitized," my father stated.

My mother and I were shocked to hear my dad opening up about his time in jail.

"Well, now that's in the past, and we should move on to the future!" exclaimed my mother.

After lunch we all took a stroll around the neighborhood.

"I just want to walk around, and feel the sun and breath the fresh air!" he exclaimed.

The neighbors were all suspiciously peeking out from behind their windows at us, as we walked by. They were surprised to see my father out of jail and walking about freely. Mrs. Bugnacki, who just so happened to be outside watering her pansies, turned around and squirted herself in the face when she noticed my dad walking on her sidewalk!

"I see nothing has changed much around here!" chuckled my father.

"Well something bad happened Dad...Chomper died," I solemnly stated.

"Really? That sort of reminds me of the end of the Wizard of Oz, when the Wicked Witch is finally destroyed and her henchmen begin cheering for Dorothy!" exclaimed my father.

I shook my head in agreement.

"We both know that you had everything to do with it... Dorothy," chuckled my father.

"Yeah, I killed the Wicked Dog of the West!" I exclaimed.

We strolled back to our house, and we all just sat around and watched TV for part of the afternoon. It was so good to have my dad back home.

But for some pesky reason my mother kept asking me where Marco was, and that I should go over to his house for a while and help him do something.

Hmm, I sort of felt as if she was trying to get rid of me.

Marco is not going to be happy about me leaving home for college. We had a lot of plans for this summer.

I guess I should go over there, and break the news to him.

"Okay, okay, I'll go to Marco's. I guess I have a lot to tell him, about what's happening," I said.

"Yes, you should, and make sure you call to let us know when you will be on your way home," my father replied.

Then my parents goofily gazed at each other and giggled.

Chapter 30

I walked out the door, picked up my bike, and headed to the trail in the woods that lead to Marco's house.

So much was spinning around in my mind.

Graduating from high school and attending Caltech. Discovering that I'm a freaking genius, and getting my driver's license and a brand new Corvette convertible! I felt like singing "Zippity doo dah!" as I rode through the woods along the trail. But then my stomach sank, and I thought about Kelly Mosely and Crystal.

How could I be so smart, but be so stupid when it came to girls?

Marco's father once confided with us and graciously shared three of his precious pearls of wisdom about women. I think it was his rendition of the birds and the bees. He said...

"Boyz, three things yuz should know about women.

Number 1... If yaz wants ta understand a broad...youz got to be a shrink. It's impasta-ble for a man to ever say da right thing for a skirt's ears. Like I would say to a broad...

"Hey cream puff, howz about some Bada Bing, Bada Boom?"

Ta youz and me, dat sounds pretty romantic, right?

But to a broad it's not gonna get you nowherez.

Dey want youz to take em out ta Pizza Hut',..bring em flowaz,... tell em' how smokin' hot dey look.

Then you can drop the 'Bada Bing, Bada Boom!!'" he smugly stated.

"What about Number 2 Dad?!" Marco eagerly begged.

"Okay boyz, here's Number 2...

Neva', and I mean neva', eva' let a broad know youz is smarta' den her! Which of course is very difficult to do, since every man knowz we is "Gean yus is"!

Alwayz tell dem dey is "right", and youz'll never have an argument wid a broad.

Like dis... Say youz are at da strip club all night wid your piazzano's, and you roll in about 2 AM. Your old lady is steamin' mad because she made dinna for yaz, on account it waz ya weddin' anniversary.

"What kind of stupid schmuck forgets it's their wedding anniversary!" she sez as she blows her bleached blonde hair stack.

"Awe youz right hot buns, I am a stupid schmuck" sez me.

"Your friends are a bunch of morons, and you better stop hanging around at that disgusting strip club!" sez da wife.

"Youz is right luscious lips, doze guys are morons, and I'll never go back to dat stinkin' strip club again. By da way doll face, youz looks beautiful when youz is pissed off at me," sez me.

"I do!? Well then…I guess I'll forgive you, let's go to bed you stud!" sez da skirt.

"Bada Bing, Bada boom!" rejoiced Mr. D.

"What about Number 3 Dad?" salivated Marco.

"Well boys, take it from me. Broads love it when youz give dem condiments".

For example; "Hey doll, ya puss looks pretty good with that make up goop all over it, now go get me a brew," or

"Hey baby, wid a body like you got, I could make a few bucks turnin' you out workin' the street corners!".

And one of my personal favorites;

"Youz got a hot rack ya sexy slut, now howz about some Bada Bing, Bada Boom!"

Communicationz like dat, iz alwayz a home run wid da broads, boyz!" he confidently stated.

Maybe Mr. D was right.

"To understand women you do need to be a Shrink."

From now on... I'm going to take his advice on women.

Chapter 31

I could see Marco's house in the distance, and I couldn't wait to tell him the news about my dad coming home and Caltech.

As I approached his house, I noticed his bike was lying on his lawn, but there were no cars in the driveway.

His father's black Cadillac and his mother's pink Thunderbird were gone. This could be the perfect time to watch those dirty movies he was telling me about!

I tossed my bike on their lawn and began frantically knocking on the door.

After a bit of knocking, I could hear his footsteps coming towards the door and fumbling with the sticky lock.

"Hurry up! I want to watch those X rated porno movies of your sexy luscious stepmom before they get home!" I shouted.

The door began to slowly creak open, and there I was, standing face to face with Mrs. Delgato, and all she was wearing was her short pink satin robe, and a purple feathered belt.

"Well hello Dawny, what a pleasant surprise," she flirtatiously stated. Then she took me by the hand, and led me into the living room.

I was praying that maybe she didn't hear the part about "watching her dirty porno movies and sexy luscious stepmom".

"Sit down Dawnny, make yourself at home. Can I get ya somethin' to drink?" she seductively asked.

And then she pushed me down on the couch!

"Maybe a glass of wa,water please," I stuttered.

She smiled, and turned toward the kitchen and she slithered away. It was very apparent to me that she had nothing on underneath her tiny satin pink robe.

My heart began pounding like Indian war drums as I nervously sat there looking around the room and waited for her return.

I nervously looked around the room and suddenly noticed right in front of me, hanging on the wall a large black and white photograph of Mr. Delgato, making an angry face with his fist in the air. I tried not to look at it, since some things are worth dying for!

I could hear the clinking of glassware coming from the kitchen. The freezer door opening and the rumbling of ice cubes before the freezer door was slammed shut. And then the water faucet turned on and off. All my senses were switched to DEFCON 1! Full alert!

"Is, is Marco home?" I nervously shouted out.

She slowly sauntered toward me, holding my icy glass of water, and I noticed that the purple feather sash that was previously tying her robe closed was now untied and just dangling! She was holding her robe closed with her left hand as she bent over and handed me the glass of water!

"No sweethot, Marco and his fatha drove to LA for a ball game. They won't be back for a lawng...lawng...time. I'm so lonely though.

They left me here all alone, with no one ta play with," she lustfully replied.

Then she reached her slender fingers, with her long press on golden finger nails into my glass, and removed an ice cube. She stared into my eyes as she smeared the ice cube along her forehead and face, before she began sucking on it with her voluptuous beacho lips!

"It's a hawt luscious one taday...isn't it Dawny?" she seductively stated.

My brains, Cingulate cortex, Amygdala and Insula, were pumping out massive amounts of "Let's get it on baby!" into my bloodstream!

What would Mr. D. say right now??

"Uhh, you're so right Mrs. D, you are always so right! Uhm, your tail looks very pretty today!" I nervously stated.

She gazed at me oddly, then disregarded it and got back to business. She moved in closer and sat down next to me on the couch. Leaning into me, I could feel her hot body pressing on me, and that's when I started to hyperventilate!

"Just relax Dawny, what I'm gonna do to ya is gonna make ya wildest dreams come true," she whispered.

And then she dropped her hand that was holding her robe closed, revealing everything that was lurking behind that thin layer of pink satin!

I swallowed hard as she moved in on me, and she straddled on my lap. Sweat began drenching my body as she began kissing and licking me on the neck! All I could hear was my heart thumping like a jackhammer! I closed my eyes and all I could envision was Chomper humping on old lady Bugnacki's Bambi statuary!

She continued kissing my neck, and her hands began roaming all over my body!

"I heard ya say somethin' about watching the dirty movies I was in?" she lustfully whispered in my ear.

"Uh, well, I, uh," I stammered.

My senses were going into complete overload, and my testosterone gauge was red lining as she began deeply kissing me on the mouth, and shoving her tongue in too! Since I had never made out before, I was just reciprocating back what she was doing to me, and I think I was doing pretty good!

She began moaning and writhing on my lap and then she began unbuttoning my shirt as she clenched the hair on the back of my head with her other hand! Her robe was wide open and she asked me to touch her. I was paralyzed as she was mauling me, then she reached over, and took hold of my wrist, and began moving my hand all over her naked body, sliding it across her chest then downward to her stomach.

I felt her belly button as she placed my finger in it! I used up my last synapse of brain neurons to register,

"Oh, she has an innie," in my mind.

"This is so much better than watching an old dirty movie, isn't it Dawny?" she seductively whispered.

"Right, again Mrs. D!" I whispered back.

My heart was pumping blood at a rate equivalent to sub atomic particles traveling faster than the speed of light! We were going at it like wild animals, and then she whispered something to me.

"What do you think about me, Dawny?" she lustfully questioned, as she was caressing my stomach with her long press on fingernails.

She continued kissing my neck, then my chest, and then slowly working her way down to my stomach as we were passionately groping each other.

She was expertly kissing and licking my sweaty skin,

"Mmmm...salty," she savored.

Then she completely removed her scant robe and began ripping off my clothes!

"Mmmm, that's better. Now tell me what you really think of me, and I'll go all the way," she licked her lips and lewdly whispered.

I couldn't think of anything else to say except "I love your Scungilli!".

"Com' awn Dawny...It'll make me so horny," she moaned.

I could feel her crispy artificial blonde hair on my belly as it swept over my bare skin!

"If you really want me to keep going down, just tell me what you think of me...," she whispered.

I could feel her hot breath on my stomach as she spoke to me. My mind was fried as I tried to maintain some inkling of composure and thought.

"Come on! Say somethin'!!" she demanded.

I struggled to think! I didn't know what to say but I finally remembered what Mr. D had told us…

"Mrs. D…You're…you're a hot piece of ass," I proudly stated.

Suddenly it was as if a train robber had pulled the brake lever on an old steam train, and all the wheels were locking up as a long trail of hot sparks trailed off from the braking iron wheels, as it screeched down the tracks to a complete stop! Mrs. D looked up at me sternly.

"Did you just say I was a piece of ass?!" she dreadfully exclaimed.

I didn't know what to say, but I knew I had to be a Shrink to salvage this!

"You are right Mrs. D, but I meant it in a complementary way. Like, you are a beautiful, sophisticated woman," I pleaded.

She stared at me intensely for a moment, as she processed what I had just said.

"You think I'm beautiful?" she modestly inquired.

"Oh yes, gorgeous!" I replied. I couldn't believe it! I was actually pulling this back together! She smiled and slowly eased back into her passion groove and returned to kissing and licking my stomach again!

"Tell me what else you think about me Dawny and I'll go awllll the way down," she whispered and moaned.

I could feel my eyes rolling around in my head, and I was in some sort of paralysis due to the lack of blood that had left my upper body!

"C'om on Dawny," she erotically whispered.

I could feel her hot breath on me down there as she was opening her mouth and slowly licking her lips!

"C'om on Dawny…talk dirty to me, and I'll rock your world," she begged.

I tried to think of something, but there was no blood left in my brain! I understood that she was looking for more "condiments," and I had better be quick about it, otherwise she might change her mind and stop!

"Think harder!!" I ordered my Cingulate cortex!!

Then it suddenly hit me!! I remembered Mr. Delgato's genius guidance!

It was as if Marco's father had whispered the seductive words into my ear of how to seduce his wife, and I listened! It became so clear to me, and now I was confident that I now had in my grasp the golden words that Mrs. D's starving horny body has been aching and yearning to feast on. She will be putty in my hands and going all the way with me in a matter of seconds!

"Mrs. D… Yaz got a hot rack, ya sexy slut!, howz about some Badda bing badda boom," I arrogantly whispered.

Chapter 32

I slowly rode my bike down the trail back toward my house.

I thought quietly to myself about the unlucky situations that I've encountered with girls lately. It seems nothing has been going my way. But I learned something else about women today.

Never take advice about women from Mr.Delgado…

"EVER!!!!"

Chapter 33

Senator Blackstone returned the following Monday morning with a large manila envelope in his hand.

When he knocked on our front door, my father answered it.

"Hello Mr. Lord, I'm Senator Blackstone. You must be very proud of your boy!" he stated.

My father became a little nervous talking to the Senator, since his time in jail made him very resentful of anyone wearing a suit. He said they all look like lawyers, and it was lawyers that put him in jail.

They shook hands, and my father invited the Senator into the house.

"So it seems you are interested in my son's brain," my father chuckled.

"Yes, we have some big plans for your brain child," he replied, and he winked at me.

He then opened up the envelope, and there were two copies of a legal contract.

"Why don't we sit down at the kitchen table, and we can go over this "Agreement". I'll do my best to explain what it means, and if you are comfortable with it, we can wrap this up today," stated the Senator.

"To be honest with you sir, I'm a little puzzled why the government is so interested in Donny. I'm sure you have a large inventory of over qualified government stooges that you can tap into. What do you really want out of Donny?" my father curiously questioned.

The Senator loosened his tie a bit, and thought for a moment.

"You are right Mr. Lord, there are plenty of other college kids, professors, and government "stooges" we could tap into. Some are exceptionally smart. Some are even geniuses, but very few of them are "Super Geniuses" like your boy, Donny.

We believe that in time, he will become a world famous research scientist. Maybe someday he will find cures for diseases like cancer and multiple sclerosis.

Maybe someday he will even develop drugs that will double a person's life expectancy or help a crippled child to walk again. We believe your son has a gift, and we want to make sure he has everything he needs at his disposal to flourish. We want him for the good of the people of the United States of America, and the world," stated the Senator.

My father rubbed his face the way he usually did when he was either confused or freaking out.

"What if you are wrong about him, and he doesn't meet your expectations? Are you going to throw him out of Caltech, take his money back, and throw me back in jail?!" my father exclaimed.

I sat there quietly, as my father interrogated the Senator. But I wondered, was my father more concerned about me failing and getting kicked out of school, or because he would get thrown back into jail?

I was sure it was the latter. My father never really seemed to care much about me until I could be of some use to him, like making his drugs.

"Here Mr. Lord, let's look over the contract, and I think it will answer all of your questions," stated the Senator.

We all sat down at the kitchen table, and my mother had made some coffee for the men.

Senator Blackstone handed my father one of the copies and together we read through each line. It was very clear.

My father gets out of Prison. They are to provide me with my High School Diploma with Valedictorian honors and a California Driver's license.

The Senator casually reached into his pocket, and pulled out a small square paper card which was my driver's license. My name and address were already printed on it!

I also get a full scholarship to the California Institute of Technology, including room and board.

They will pay me twenty five thousand dollars per year for year one, and year two. Fifty thousand dollars per year for year three, and four, and so on.

I also get a brand new 1969 Stingray Corvette convertible (choice of color).

The contract term begins July 1, 1969 and will expire July 1,1979. After the contract expires, there is an option to continue working for the government with an increased salary negotiation. Or, I can choose to leave and work somewhere else. However all patents and works in progress are the property of the United States Government. Then came the fine print:

In the event that Donny Lord fails to produce exponentially and/or refuses to follow orders of/about the creation/development of products/serum/drugs   vital to the government's interests as so pertaining to. The government and its agencies here by reserve the right to terminate this contract without said notice.

"Everything is fine until I got to the fine print! It doesn't say anything about me NOT going back to jail!" my father exclaimed.

The Senator leaned back in his chair, and intertwined his fingers together across his stomach.

"That's right Mr. Lord. If Donny doesn't do what we need him to do, he will get kicked out of Caltech after 4 years. But you will be immediately returned to finish off your sentence exactly where you left off. It's a little motivational insurance policy the boys down at the bureau conjured up," smugly stated the Senator.

"That's bullshit!" my father shouted.

"Look Mr. Lord, we don't really anticipate that happening, since your son is very, very bright. It's just a minor technicality. The higher ups just wanted it in there to cover their butts," replied the Senator.

"A minor technicality?! You have a lot more confidence in my kid than I do!" exclaimed my father.

I was really taken aback by his condescending comment. He really has no idea of who I am, or what I can do. All he ever was really concerned about was his precious drugs, and making money on the LSD that he forced me to make.

My dad never threw a ball with me, or had taken me to a baseball game like Marco's father.

We all just sat there at the kitchen table in silence, until Senator Blackstone picked up a pen, and handed it to my father.

"You can either sign it now, and be happy for your kid and stay out of jail, hopefully for good. Or, if you don't sign it, you can go back to San Quentin tonight, and your kid can go back to making cherry bombs in your basement," grinned the Senator.

My father paused and sternly stared at the Senator for a moment. Then he snatched the pen from him and recklessly signed the contract. My mother took the pen and then she signed it. Even though I was a minor, I signed it too.

The Senator then collected the paperwork, and informed us that a correspondent from the "Agency" will be calling to set up the program for me.

"When do I get my Corvette!" I exclaimed.

"It will be waiting for you in Pasadena, kid," he replied.

My father hastily got up without shaking the Senators hand, and he left the room as my mother began cleaning up the table.

"Come on Donny, walk with me to my car," said the Senator.

"You must be really excited about your new adventure. I'll be checking in on you from time to time. Here is my card. If you need anything, don't hesitate to call me.

When you get to Caltech, you will be surrounded by some of the most brilliant people in the world. They may feel threatened and intimidated by your presence, and may not be so nice to you. Go with your gut, and don't let closed minded professors or students tell you that "It can't be done, or it's impossible".

We are counting on you Donny to do some remarkable things, and the sooner you get started, the better," he stated.

He shook my hand, then got into his car firmly holding the manila envelope.

He rolled down the window, reached inside his jacket pocket and removed a long white envelope.

"I almost forgot kid...here is an advance on your pay so you can get some of the things you might need for school," said the Senator.

I took the envelope and saw it was filled with hundred dollar bills!

"Thank you Senator Blackstone! I'll do my best to make you proud of me," I exclaimed.

"I know you will son," he replied, and he started his car and drove away.

My mother came outside, and put her arm over my shoulders as we watched the Senator drive off down the street.

"Now that you have your driver's license, let's go for a drive to Dairy Queen. You'll need all the practice driving you can get before you leave," she chuckled.

She then handed me my brand new driver's license card. I didn't know what was more exciting to me, leaving home and going to Caltech, or driving my parents 57 Chevy Belair to Dairy Queen!

I jumped into the driver's seat and my mother got in on the passenger side. I carefully placed the key into the ignition and turned it. The car's engine struggled a few revolutions before it kicked over.

It wasn't the first time I had ever driven a car. My father used to put me on his lap, and let me steer around town when I was a kid. I think that counts as "driving".

I carefully shifted the car into reverse, and we slowly rolled out of the driveway.

"Next time look both ways before you back out into the street," mother rudely commented.

"Oh, oh ya sure thing mom," I replied.

I placed the car into drive and slowly drove toward the north end of the street.

Wait till those degenerate losers see ME driving my parents Belair. This is so cool!

As we traveled down the street at 10 MPH, I noticed Ricky Johnson throwing a tennis ball onto his dilapidated roof, and catching it as it rolled back down. He suddenly stopped, and stared at me in amazement, as his eyes tracked me all the way down the street. He must have thought I was really slick, and really cruisin!

"Why did you go this way? It would have been a lot closer if you would have gone the other way, and turned down State street," my mother scolded.

Hmm, that's the second time she made a disparaging remark about my driving.

"I think it's the same distance either way mom," I cautiously replied.

We approached a stop sign, and she ordered me to take a right turn onto Jupiter lane.

"Mom, it's faster if I go to the left, and go down the Boulevard," I insisted.

"No, go to the right, there is one less traffic light this way!" she insisted.

"I'm doing the driving, I'll go the way I think is better!" I shot back.

I punched the gas pedal and took the left turn!

My mother just sat there fuming, as we headed down the Boulevard. Just then I noticed some heavy traffic ahead. There was an accident, and the traffic had come to a complete stop!

"I told you this way was no good!" she reprimanded.

"How was I supposed to know there was going to be an accident down here?" I grumbled.

"If you would have listened to me in the first place, we would be at Dairy Queen by now, some genius you are!" she sarcastically stated.

I got so agitated, I did an abrupt "U" turn so I wouldn't have to listen to her anymore! As I did it, I didn't notice the police cruiser coming out of the coffee shop adjacent to me, and I smashed into him!

"Now you've done it! They are going to take away your driver's license for sure now!" she scolded.

I just slumped over the steering wheel, and sat there as the police officer exited his car and inspected the damage. He shook his head in disbelief, then continued over to my window.

"That was an illegal "U" turn you made, boy," he arrogantly stated.

"Officer, I told him he shouldn't have gone down the Boulevard. I insisted that we go my way, down Jupiter street. There is one less traffic light, but he wouldn't listen to me!" my mother exclaimed.

I sat there in a state of mental numbness, as if I had just received a lobotomy performed on my brain by my mother.

"See, I told you this was a bad way, Mr. Know It All!" and she went on and on and on…and on. The officer asked me to get out of the car, and for my driver's license.

"You stay put Mom," he stated.

He ordered me to go to the back of his cruiser and to put my hands on the trunk. He followed behind me, and I leaned over the trunk and placed my hands down.

"Am I going to jail officer?" I fearfully asked.

"No kid, I just wanted to give you a break from your loud mouth mother. Here's some great advice I once got from an Italian mob guy I pulled over some time ago. Whenever a woman is giving you a hard time, just tell her she is right!" he sincerely stated.

"Actually Officer, I did hear about that method once before, from my friend's father who I think might be the same fellow you are referring to. But I vowed never to use advice from that gentleman again, since it caused me to get ejected out of a very heated romantic situation with a very hot woman," I disappointedly stated.

"Never mind that son, now get back into that car, and listen to me and tell your mother she was right, and see what happens," he chuckled.

I nodded my head in agreement with the officer. I would have done anything to keep myself out of jail. Telling my mother she was right was proof of that! He returned to his cruiser as I reluctantly dredged myself across the pavement, and got back into our car.

"See! If you would have listened to me you wouldn't be in this mess!" she exclaimed.

"MOM, YOU WERE RIGHT!" I shouted.

Instantly her demeanor changed and she smiled. She had a look of euphoria on her face and paused for a few seconds.

"All right, no worries. I made a few mistakes when I was your age too. Let's supersize our ice creams if we can ever get to Dairy Queen!" she giggled.

Even though it was difficult to eat crow the way I did, it seemed to put an end to her badgering.

The officer shortly returned after calling in my information on his radio.

"Everything okay here?" he sarcastically questioned.

"Just peachy officer, my son admitted "I" was right!" my mother gloated.

The officer winked at me with a nod. I was now welcomed into the brotherhood.

"Here's your license kid. You must be pretty important. When I called this in, they strictly replied "Laissez-faire". That means "Hands off the kid," in police talk. Please drive carefully, and remember what I told you," ordered the officer.

I thanked him profusely, then I started the car and we drove off.

"What did the officer say to you?" my mother inquired.

"He told me I should listen to my mother," I coyly replied.

We finally made it to Dairy Queen, but I didn't feel like such a big shot anymore driving in the Belair with my mother, especially since part of the bumper was now hanging off the car.

Afterwards, I drove home the way my mother wanted me to go, and I parked the car in our driveway.

My father was sitting outside under a tree, and was watching me as I pulled in. I walked over to sit with him on a lawn chair in the shade, and my mother rushed into the house. She was probably going to call her friends to tell them how I hit a cop car, because I didn't listen to her, and I admitted she was right.

"A) What happened to the car? and B) where the hell is my dam ice cream cone!" my father shouted.

"Dad you know what it's like driving around with mom, right?" I stated.

He leaned back in his chair, and sipped on his iced tea.

"Yep…the only thing worse than your mom's back seat driving is her cooking. She back seat drove you into delirium, huh?" he chuckled.

"Even the cop I hit felt sorry for me!" I laughed.

"You hit a cop car!" my father roared.

"Yep, but I apparently have a "Get out of Jail" free drivers license," I replied.

It suddenly got extremely quiet when I mentioned "jail". Why can't I stop saying stupid things?! UGH!!

I faintly heard the phone ring in the house, and my mother was talking to someone. A few minutes later she came out, and told me that it was a woman who called from Caltech.

"Her name is Verdi and she's originally from Cuba. You are going to be staying with her and her husband while you will be attending school there. They both work for the school as bookkeepers. She seems very nice, and she says she is looking forward to you staying with her," reported my Mom.

"She didn't want to talk to me?" I asked.

"She is going to make a list of things you are going to need, and she said she will call you this week. She also said she was going to drive up to Bakersfield to pick you up, so we don't have to drive you down to Pasadena and deal with the traffic," said my mom.

"Wow, this is really happening!" I said.

"Do you think it would be okay if I went clothes shopping with Marco? I think I'm old enough to start shopping for clothes on my own, now that I am sixteen," I hopefully stated.

"No way!" my mother abruptly exclaimed.

My father glanced at her, and gave her a nod that meant 'it was time to cut the cord'.

"Sure son, just keep the receipts," my father stated.

Chapter 34

The following morning my mom let me borrow the car, and I drove over to pick up Marco. I didn't want to go through the awkwardness of seeing Mrs. D, so I just honked the horn when I pulled into his driveway. Marco came running out of his house and he jumped into the front seat.

"This is so cool that you got your license. Maybe we can pick up a few skirts on the way home from shopping!" he exclaimed.

"Maybe we'll get lucky with the chicks who work at the store, when they see how cool we are buying clothes without our mothers," I replied.

"Where are we going?" asked Marco.

"Only to the hippest and coolest store in Bakersfield...Chess King!" I exclaimed.

Marco collapsed in his seat.

Everyone knew that Chess King was the coolest place.

"I had been there once before with my mom, but she wouldn't let me get anything. She said everything looked like clown clothes. I remember it being really dark in there, and they burned incense that smelled like pot. While all the other stores were playing elevator music, they blasted rock and roll music to get you into the buying groove.

The girls who worked there were all hippies, wearing love beads, ripped up bell bottom jeans, and supposed to be very easy," I gloriously stated.

"I heard about a kid from a kid at his school, who had told him that someone he knew, had heard of a kid who had spent $100 of his Christmas money at Chess King. The sales girl told him if he spent another $50 she would go into a dressing room and make out with him! The poor kid only had forty five bucks left!" exclaimed Marco.

Marco suddenly became quiet, and just looked out the window.

"What's the matter?" I asked.

"If I knew we were going to Chess King, I would have brought more money," he sadly stated.

"Don't worry about that," I replied.

And I reached into my pocket, and pulled out a roll of $100 bills.

"I have enough for both of us!" I laughed.

Marco couldn't believe his eyes!

"Where did you get that!?" he exclaimed.

"I have to tell you something Marco. A Senator came to visit me a few days ago. He said I'm some sort of genius, and he offered me a full scholarship to Caltech along with some other things. That's how I got my driver's license and all this money. I won't be going back to high school this fall, and I'll be leaving for Pasadena in about two weeks to start college," I quietly stated.

Marco became sad and looked down at the worn out floor.

"So when will I get to see ya?" he sadly asked.

"Oh, it's only about two hours away, I'm sure I'll be coming home all the time, and how cool will it be when you come visit me down at Caltech! College girls galore!!" I replied.

That seemed to raise Marco's spirits and he perked up again.

"But we'll also keep in touch on the phone, and write letters too. I'd like you to keep an eye on Kelly and Crystal while I'm away. I really messed things up with the both of them," I regretfully stated.

"Don't worry Donny, I'll hold down the fort," proclaimed Marco.

"You are my best friend Marco...no matter where I am," I replied.

He nodded in agreement.

"There it is!" Marco shouted.

I turned into the strip mall where Chess King was located, and we scrambled out of the car.

As we approached the store we could hear the loud rock music blasting. Marco opened the main entry door, and looked back at me in a state of ecstasy as we entered the store and passed through a long curtain of wooden beads. It was just as I expected…dark and smelly!

A very sexy "hippied out" sales girl approached us, and introduced herself.

"Hi, I'm Marcia, do you studs need any help?" she stated.

"I have a hundred and fifty dollars!" Marco blurted out.

I placed my hand over my face in embarrassment and shook my head in disbelief!

"Mmmm yummy, we love horny teenage boys that spend lots of money, so you guys are here for the Chess King 'Checkmate-ing' service are you?" she flirtatiously stated.

Marco was shaking his head erratically up and down in agreement!

"Okay, when you boys are finished shopping, I'll hook you up with Tracy and Jodi, two of my hottest coworkers," she lewdly stated and winked.

"Do we have to spend $150 each or can we combine it?" Marco salivated.

"Well that depends on if you two want a "Menage et twa" or do you each want your own personal Check Mate attendant?" she decadently replied.

Marco turned to me, and with a sorry look of despair he whispered to me...

"I only brought 8 bucks, can you spot me the rest?" he begged.

I looked at Marcia as she twirled her long messy brown hair around her middle finger. Marco was intensely staring at me with tears in his eyes as he waited for my decision. I glanced over and noticed two hot trashy hippie girls folding pants, and having a quiet conversation about them doing it with a couple of high school boys at a party the night before. I could smell their intense fragrance of strawberry perfume as it swept through the air and they were obviously checking us out too.

"Okay we are in for the $300!" I exclaimed.

Marco grabbed me, and began shaking me!

"You are the best friend a guy could ever have!" he exclaimed.

"Well then let's get shopping," said Marcia.

We immediately began buying everything from brightly colored striped bell bottom pants, colorful fringed puffy shirts, tye dye shirts, and suede vests. We even bought these really cool leather floppy hats. It seemed that the clothes were only the icing on the cake, since we were soon going to be paired up with those strawberry flavored hippie girls, Tracy and Jodi. We had accumulated two large piles of clothes at the register as Marcia began tallying up the merchandise.

"I just want to point out this sign to you boys, "NO CASH REFUNDS". It wouldn't be nice if you returned everything after you got to spend some time with Tracy and Jodi. Now, I just totaled up your purchase and you are at $296. I can't get you both in with Jodi and Tracy unless you get over the $300 "hump"," she stated and raised her eyebrows.

"Okay what do you have for $4 bucks?" I asked.

"Hmmm, we really don't have anything that cheap. The cheapest thing we have are these "Ass, Gas or Grass...nobody rides for free!" tee shirts for eight bucks," she stated.

"Perfect, my father will love it," I replied.

I peeled off three one hundred dollar bills and Marco handed me his eight bucks. I eagerly paid her, and she bagged all the clothes into two separate large bags.

"I'll leave these bags for you on the counter so you can pick them up when you are done with "Tracy and Jodi". Now you two go in the back and wait together in the big dressing room marked #1. Make sure your eyes are closed tightly and you'll have to be ready. Take off your clothes, and I'll send them in...okay!" she whispered.

Marco was basically sprinting for the dressing rooms before Marcia had finished her sentence, and I was right behind him! We were frantically undressing and knocking our elbows against the dressing room walls. I heard Marcia's voice project over the store intercom.

"Tracy and Jodi, please report to dressing room #1 for customer service on the double".

"Donny, we are going to make it with hot hippie chicks!" Marco exclaimed.

"I hope they don't have any venereal diseases, never mind I don't care!!" I whispered.

We sat there nervously waiting and fidgeting on the hard wooden bench with deep anticipation, until we heard footsteps heading toward our curtain. Then suddenly there was a knock at the door frame.

We kept our eyes closed tightly and we both chimed..."Come on in!". I felt the slight breeze of the curtains flipping open as our dates entered the dressing room.

Oddly, I didn't smell the sweet fragrance of strawberries but it was more of an "Old Spice" aroma.

We slowly opened our eyes, anxious to reveal our hot hippie girls! But instead we were mortified to see two confused burly maintenance men dressed in work clothes standing before us! Their names were embroidered on their shirt pockets. "Jodi" and "Tracy".

"Hey what's going on in here with you two perverts! If you two queers can't keep your pants on, you should get a room someplace else and keep your Homo-sapiens out of public places!" Tracy exclaimed.

It was so embarrassing!!!!

We quickly scrambled, putting on our pants, and we grabbed whatever we could carry and raced past the men! As we were running out, we grabbed our bags that were waiting for us on the counter, but had to endure hysterical laughter, and finger pointing from Marcia and her two strawberry flavored accomplices!

"Y'all come back now...lover boys!" she laughed.

Marco threw her the finger as we flew by them, but we both ridiculously became entangled in the beaded curtain as we tried to leave!

When we finally escaped the curtain, and made it to the car, I frantically reached into my pocket to get my car keys, but they were gone!

"Marco I can't find my keys! They must have fallen out in the dressing room!" I exclaimed.

I looked back at the store front, and there was Marcia standing behind the large glass window dangling my keys obnoxiously in front of her.

I didn't waste any time asking Marco to go back there. I just dropped my chin, barefoot and shirtless, and I walked back into the store, dragging my dignity behind me.

Once again, I had to pass through that blasted beaded curtain into Marcia's lair.

"Did you forget something, Romeo?" she sarcastically asked.

"Keys please," I replied.

She reluctantly reached into her pocket, and tossed them to me.

"I guess we deserved that," I solemnly stated.

"You know how many stupid idiot boys come in here believing that ridiculous story about spending $150 dollars? Too bad for you guys, my two assistants thought you two were cute and wanted to make it with you guys, until you blew it," she stated.

I shook my head in disbelief and headed back toward the beaded curtain.

"Nothing ever goes my way," I moaned.

"Hey kid! By the way, how did you get so much money?" Marsha asked.

I paused and looked back over my shoulder as I once again became entangled in the bead strands.

"I'm a Genius," I replied.

"Really?" she doubted and rolled her eyes.

"Yeah, hard to believe, huh," I responded.

As I left the Chess King I thought about the two valuable lessons I learned this week.

#1 Disregard advice or information about women from all of the Delgato men.

#2 Refer back to #1!

Chapter 35

Several days had passed, when I received a phone call from "Verdi", the woman who I'll be living with at Caltech.

She had a very heavy Cuban accent, and it was difficult to understand. But from what I could tell, she seemed phony.

I wondered how much they were paying her to be my Caltech foster mother. She has to be in it for the money.

I was hoping to move into a frat house or a dormitory in the not so distant future. But for now, this will have to do.

She informed me that she was very excited to have me stay with her, and she asked me what I like to eat. It was difficult to understand her with her heavy Cuban accent.

"How ju feel about Cuban food?" she asked.

"I'll eat anything as long as it doesn't look like it did while it was still alive," I joked

"Du ju like Empanadas ?" she asked.

"No, I never eat Bananas," I replied.

"Not Bananas...Empanadas! " she insisted.

I didn't know what the hell she was talking about. Finally she just gave up and changed the subject.

"Can I bring my chemistry set with me?" I asked.

"Jes, bring whatever ju want, but I don tink ju are gonna need it. Dey set ju up with some stuff already. Jus don't forget jor research notes and formulas. Everyting you need to continue yur research here at Caltech," she stated.

I thought that was a little odd, what business was it of hers that I should bring my notes and records.

"Oookay I will," I sarcastically replied.

"Good, I will be der next Saturday to pick ju up around noon, so have ready everyting ju need."

"Okay Verdi, thank you…I look forward to staying with you and your husband," I said.

"Ju are welcome, but my husband is gone now. He went back to Cuba, so it will be only me," she replied.

Then she hung up the phone.

Just me and her? Great, her husband didn't take off to Cuba because she was a hottie. She must be a real beast.

Chapter 36

The following two weeks quickly passed.

I stayed close to home since I had a lot of catching up to do with my dad.

It's funny, but he has been wearing that "Ass, Grass or Gas...Nobody Rides for Free" tee shirt ever since I gave it to him. My mom isn't amused though.

One day he was wearing it when we went to McDonalds for lunch and a very attractive woman jokingly asked him for a ride!

He asked her if she had any money, and she said "Nooo". Then he asked her if she had any grass, and she said, "Noooo."

"Well that only leaves one thing left on the list," he joked.

Then my mother barged in and told the woman to get lost! Funny thing was, after that day, that shirt was nowhere to be found. My mother claims the dryer must have eaten it along with a bunch of single socks that we could never find!

Tomorrow is finally the day I'm leaving for college.

It sounds funny to hear that, I'm actually going to college. Verdi called a few days ago, and told me she was going to arrive around lunch time and I should be ready to go.

I was starting to get a little anxious about leaving. I had never been away from home, and I was having second thoughts about it.

Though, I knew that if I didn't go, my father would be returned to prison, and I couldn't let that happen.

My clothes were all packed neatly into a large duffle bag that my dad had bought several years ago. If I needed anything else, I certainly had the money to buy whatever I wanted.

I decided to wear one of my new Chess King outfits to impress Verdi when she arrived.

She's probably expecting me to look like a geek. Wait till she gets a load of me sporting my bright red bell bottoms, my puffy purple pirate shirt, my suede floppy hat and my huge peace sign medallion. She's going to think I am so cool!

My mom decided to throw me a going away party.

Marco came over for dinner, and my mother made a frozen pizza for us.

When she opened up the box it rolled off the counter, and she had to chase it across the floor to catch it!

After she finally caught it, she placed it into the oven, not realizing that first you were supposed to take the plastic wrapping off of it, and it started to melt all over the pizza. She was able to get most of the wrapper off in time, before it totally caught on fire, but there were still little bits of burnt pieces mingling around in the cheese.

When it came out of the oven, it sort of took on a life of its own.

The pizza was bellowing up and down as if it was a breathing alien organism from outer space!

Marco tried to disguise his disdain for that extraterrestrial pizza, and gave me a "horrified" look whenever my mother wasn't looking.

My father joined us at the table as Marco and I sat there with our elbows on the table and our hands on our cheeks, bewilderedly staring at "The Thing".

My father picked up the pizza cutter, and began criss-crossing it diagonally across the pizza. When he was done, the only thing that was cut was the cheese and the remaining pieces of the wrapper.

The pizza was harder than concrete and the cutter couldn't penetrate it!

My father became alarmed, when the pizza seemed to be crawling around the table on its own. He dove on top of it and tried to break it, but it was as hard as a rock! He began hitting it on the corner of the table! He still couldn't break it and the corner of our hard wood kitchen table broke off!

"What the hell kind of pizza is this! This is harder than the rocks we had to break in the chain gang at San Quentin!" my father exclaimed.

My mother ducked away into the kitchen, but we heard a faint explanation.

"It was on sale...buy one, get one free," she reported.

"Quick, let's get out of here! There's another one of these things living in our freezer," I joked.

"Open the front door, Donny," My father ordered.

My father cautiously carried the pizza to the front door. He began spinning and spinning as if he was preparing to throw a discus, and then he launched that pizza right out the front door! Marco and I were watching in amazement as it spun and accelerated across the street! It then began hooking over toward Mrs. Bugnackis yard, and was heading right at her concrete Bambi statuary!

We watched motionlessly as it flew like a flying saucer, and its built-in guidance device was locked onto Bambi!

A loud "Thud" resonated as the pizza crashed into the statuary, and decapitated poor Bambi's head clean off!

My father quickly closed the door and pulled the shade down as Mrs. Bugnacki jumped up and peered out her window to see what the noise was all about.

"Everyone, get into the car!...We're going to Pizza Hut!" my father angrily shouted.

Marco and I raced to the back seat of the Bel Air as my father got in and started the car. We waited patiently as my mother dragged herself out of the house and slowly walked to the car. She slowly opened the door and got into the front passenger seat and turned to my father,

"Take State street, it's two minutes faster".

Chapter 37

I stood near the window, watching down the street for Verdi to arrive.

It was almost noon, and I was anxious.

I was really hoping that she was coming with my new Corvette, but my bubble burst when I noticed a Ford station wagon with fake wood paneling (Just like Kenny's car), slowly careening down our street, and searching for house numbers on the mailboxes.

The car slowly stopped in front of our house and then pulled into our driveway. The car jerked to a halt, and the engine was shut off. I could hear the loud irritating squeak and clank of the rusty door hinge as she opened her door. A slender petite woman exited the car, and headed up the walk to our front door.

She was very pretty and had long black hair that was covered with a bright floral scarf. Her bright red lipstick and large black Ray Bans made her look very mysterious and sexy.

She was wearing a white cotton sundress with a wide red belt with tall black patent leather stiletto shoes to top it off.

I observed her from behind our window curtain as she walked, and I noticed she had a swift and extremely confident rigid gait about her. I interpreted it as a "Don't even think of messing with me, or I will kill you," sort of strut.

When she finally knocked on the door, I called my parents and my mother opened the door. She introduced herself as Verdi, and my mother called me out.

I pretended to not know she was there and acted surprised when I came to the door.

"Hi, I'm Donny," I stated.

She reached out her hand, and very firmly shook my hand to the point that I thought she may have broken it.

"I'm Verdi. Lez get jur tings in da car. No time to chit chat, we have da long ride back to Pasadena, and da traffic gets worser as da day goes by," she stated.

"I sort of thought that maybe you would drive my new Corvette to pick me up," I disappointedly stated.

"Crazy kid! Der is no trunk in dat ting...comprende? Where ju going to put jour tings? On da roof!" she joked.

We went back to her car, and my father helped me load my bag and boxes into the back of the station wagon. My mother kept reminding me of things to remember while I was getting ready to leave.

Then, I hugged my parents goodbye, and it was time to leave.

"Call us tonight, okay Donny!" my mother insisted.

I nodded, and headed over to the passenger door.

"Hey! Ju drive kid," she ordered and she tossed me the keys.

"I don't feel like drivin' no more," she stated.

I was excited to drive, and eagerly raced around the car to the driver's seat. I instantly noticed a fat smoldering cigar in the ashtray, and the heavy odor of tobacco looming in the car.

"Didn't she say her husband was gone?" I thought as I closed the squeaky door and started the car.

She had some final words with my parents then walked over to the passenger side, and got into the car.

She didn't just sit normally though, but sideways with her back to me, and was totally facing outwards as if she was watching for someone.

I gently backed the car out of the driveway and we were off to Pasadena.

She stayed perched, watching out the side window as she dictated directions to me. It wasn't until we had made it onto the expressway that she turned and sat normally. She constantly looked in the rear view mirror as if to see if someone was following us.

Then she reached down to the ashtray, and lit up that cigar!

I was totally floored to see a woman smoking a cigar.

"Wats a matter. Ju never see a beautiful woman smoking a chigar?" she questioned.

I just kept looking straight, and drove on as I shook my head in disbelief.

"Man, this lady is one tough bitch," I thought.

We drove for about an hour, until she seemed to notice something unusual, while looking in the rear view mirror.

"Pull off da nex exit!" she ordered.

I pulled off, and she directed me to take a few short turns which ended us up in the parking lot of a large furniture store.

"Drive around de back, and stop when I tell ju to," she ordered.

I was really confused since this obviously wasn't the way to Pasadena.

I slowly drove along the side of the long store and she directed me to turn left at the end of the building. I continued driving along the back side of the store, passing all sorts of broken furniture and old stained mattresses that were stacked against it.

"Keep going to de end, and make a left turn at de end of da building!" she ordered.

We were making a complete horseshoe traveling around the concrete block store.

I made the final turn around the end of the building, and after we traveled about 20 feet along the building wall, she ordered me to stop the car.

Then, she suddenly began hiking up her sexy white cotton sundress!

"Oh Geez, here we go! She couldn't wait any longer to seduce me!" I thought.

"Don't you think we should wait until we get back to your place to make love?" I eagerly questioned.

She just blankly stared at me through her dark sunglasses, and reached down between her smooth naked thighs.

"Okay, never mind. Now's a good time! So you're not going to ask me, what I think of you? Are you?" I joked.

She began jostling her hands about under her dress, and it seemed as if she was having difficulty removing her underwear!

My heart began to pound as she was urgently lifting and tugging under her dress and wrestling with her lingerie!

I was beginning to lean over to kiss her when I thought she was finally done removing her underwear, but instead of pulling off her panties, she revealed a very large black automatic pistol that had been secretly holstered to her inner thigh!

She quickly jumped out of the car, and patiently waited at the back corner of the building with her gun held between her two hands, as she was peeking around the corner!

A moment later, I could hear the sound of a car's engine that was slowly rolling on the loose gravel coming up behind us! Suddenly the nose of a long black Cadillac sedan began to turn the corner behind us.

Verdi quickly jumped out in front of the car and poised herself in an execution style stance as she raised her big black pistol up and began rapidly pulling the trigger!

"BANG! BANG! BANG! BANG! BANG! The shots echoed through the parking lot, and I couldn't believe what was happening!

She shot the windshield of the Cadillac to pieces!

Then she "matter of factly" stepped aside as the black sedan accelerated and crashed into a large metal dumpster! She fired another bullet into the sedans gas tank, then she casually lowered her gun, and got back in the car and threw her cigar into the puddle of gas leaking from the gas tank.

"Go!" she ordered as the Cadillac caught fire behind us!

I froze as I gazed into my rear view mirror.

I saw two dead men slumped over in their seats. Their faces were covered in blood, and their bodies were shot to pieces!

She reached down, and opened the glove compartment, and she calmly took out another cigar and lit it.

"Go! I say!" she scolded.

I was freaking out! I had never seen a dead human before, but I put my foot to the metal and managed to quickly accelerate!

As we left the parking lot, we heard a loud explosion when the sedan's gas tank blew up and I left a black strip of rubber on the road leaving the parking lot!

Within a few minutes we were back on the freeway, and again heading to Pasadena.

"Why did you kill those men!?" I exclaimed.

"Okay kid, der are some tings you are going to need to know dat dey have been keeping ju in da darkness about. I am not a bookkeeper. I am an agent for da CIA, assigned to keep ju safe. My real name is Sofia. Verdi is how ju say, my "nickname". It is less for "El Verdugo". I am known as "De Assassin," I kill bad people for fun," she smugly bragged.

"Doez guys back dere were Russian KGB. Dey were trying to kidnap ju and smuggle ju back to Russia. Dey found out about ju from a spy who was in de prison wid jur father. His name was Stanislav. Jur father told him ju were a "science geek" and you made some crazy chit, "Da Silver Orchid" my boss called it," she said.

"The Silver Orchid? What the hell is that!" I exclaimed.

"It's der code name for "makes you get old fast". Da government has big plans for it, and de Russians are after it too," she replied.

"Whatever it is kid, it must be big time and people are gonna die trying to get to ju. I am here to protect ju and keep ju safe. The boss will be in contact wid ju when dey tink ju are ready," she stated.

It was too much for me to comprehend. But I realized that there was more to this scholarship thing than working for the government. My life was now in danger.

Chapter 38

We soon arrived on campus, and Verdi directed me to a little inconspicuous two story brick building behind the science department.

"Here we are. Now park in da back, and we will bring jour tings in," she ordered.

I drove down a narrow driveway that ended in a secluded parking lot behind the building.

We unloaded the car, and she helped me carry my things up to the second floor of the building.

To my amazement, there was a full laboratory set up along with a large living quarters attached to it.

"Jour room is on da right," she stated, and she dropped my bags on the floor.

Then she picked up the phone that was hanging on the wall, and dialed a phone number.

I watched her concerned look as she waited for someone to answer.

She began talking to what seemed to be her supervisor, it was in some sort of code and I couldn't understand it.

I'm sure in time I will figure it out though. I think she was detailing the hit she had put on those Russian guys.

I moved my things into my room where there was a large desk, and three large bookcases containing hundreds of volumes of scientific textbooks.

My bed was small, but there was a brand new color TV set, and a Hi-fi stereo radio-record player in the room.

As I scanned the book case, I noticed a certain book on the shelf labeled "Organic Chemistry".

I don't know why I was drawn to it, maybe it was the color of the book or the style of the text on the binder, but I pulled it out and I began reading it.

Amazingly, things were becoming clearer to me. I read the entire book by midnight, and comprehended it completely. Verdi came into my room and asked me if I was hungry.

I was so busy reading, I totally forgot about food.

"Do you have any Hamburger D'Lux or Chef Boyardee?" I asked.

"Dat stuff, ju can go into da lab, and make jorself with da chemicals...If ju want some real food, I have a Cuban sandwich I tink ju will like," she stated.

"Can I ask you something, Verdi? How is it that you are from Cuba, and you are working for the United States CIA? Aren't you a Commie or something?" I asked.

"A lot of Cubans don't like Castro kid. I am proud to be an American and fight for dis country. I'll go make ju an Empanadas now," she stated, and she left my room.

"Gee, I thought I told you I didn't like Bananas!" I shouted to the kitchen.

Crap! I just realized I forgot to call my mother!

"Verdi, where is the phone, I have to call my mother!" I shouted.

She quickly returned carrying a desk phone that was attached to a long cord.

"Hey kid ju can call jur momma, but no talk about what happened today or what's going on here. Just tell her everyting is great...ju got it Mang?" she firmly stated.

I quickly dialed the number and my mother instantly answered the phone.

"Donny, what the hell! I was worried sick!" she exclaimed.

"Sorry Mom, it took me a while to settle in and unpack. I'll get you the number here so you can call me," I said.

"Okay, it's late. I'll let you go to bed, good night Donny," stated my mother.

"Goodnight Mom, and say goodnight to Dad too," I said.

"Oh! How are your living quarters and are you eating?" she quickly asked.

"It's big Mom, and I have a huge lab connected to our apartment, and yes, I ate. I'm really tired...I'll talk to you tomorrow, Mom," I sleepily stated.

"Okay, Good night Donny...I love you".

"Me too Mom," and I hung up the phone.

Verdi was standing outside my door listening.

"Ju did good kid," she stated.

"By the way, why didn't I see my Red Corvette parked outside, it's supposed to be here," I said.

"Oh ju want yur car? Right now? Hold on, I'll get it for ju".

Verdi walked into her bedroom, and returned with a small box, and she tossed it on my bed. It was a scale plastic model kit of a 1969 Corvette!

"Are you kidding me! It is supposed to be a real Corvette!" I exclaimed.

"I guess ju should have stip-ul-ju-alated dat in jor contract. Welcome to deworld of getting screwed by die government kid!" she laughed.

"Man, this is lame," I disappointedly stated as I shook my head in disbelief.

"After we learned about die Russians, da bosses felt dat it wouldn't be such a good idea to turning ju loose in a flashy red car. Dat would draw way to mucho attention. In a few months if tings are working out, ju can hit dem up for it again," she suggested.

"I guess you have a point," I replied, and I tossed the model in the garbage can.

Chapter 39

The next morning "Verdi" escorted me around campus, and brought me to meet some of my new professors. Most of which were really nice but this one guy, a chemistry professor...not so much. His name was Professor Prygocci. He was an older man with long gray unmanaged hair that seemed for the most part to be standing up wildly in all directions. He seemed very nervous and flustered as he fumbled with his paperwork and notebooks.

"You look too young to be in my chemistry class," he rudely commented.

"I'm tiny, but I'm mighty," I comically replied. He blankly stared at me and wasn't impressed.

"Listen junior, let's get one thing straight!

I'm not going to be your babysitter nor your ass wiper! You think you're some sort of boy wonder.

Actually, compared to me, you are a tidbit of mitochondrial excrement! You will never, ever, even remotely enjoy the possibility of entering into my realm of my accomplishments, achievements and total academic greatness.

As far as I'm concerned you are a waste of a desk, and my time!

Unfortunately for you, you are nothing and always will be a nothing. The one thing you WILL BE is a complete failure and embarrassment to yourself and your family!

Your first day of class is tomorrow. You should pack your bags and run home now. But if you are dumb enough to stick around, don't bother ever asking me for help! I'm going to do everything I can to get you thrown out of here. Do you still feel "mighty" now punk?!" he barked.

He then charged out of the room, pushing me aside.

"I don't think that guy likes me," I noted to Verdi.

"One dey, I'm gonna beat da chit outa dat guy!" Verdi scoffed.

"Dat guy got a biggy cheep on hiss shoulder!" I stated in my attempted Cuban accent.

Verdi continued showing me around to my classes, and introduced me to the other staff and the Dean of the school. However, she never left me unguarded and was always scanning for any potential threats.

An unfortunate custodian who was sweeping the floor, closed the lock on an open locker. The clicking sound caused Verdi to draw her gun on the poor man!

It sure did sound as if he was cocking a weapon, and the custodian ran away and hid in a broom closet!

I continued reading every day and night. Drenching myself in knowledge. As time went on, I began learning more than I could ever imagine. Best of all, I was beginning to figure things out. Things were becoming clearer and simpler to me. I knew all of the answers in class, and was becoming an encyclopedia of scientific facts.

Whatever I read, I never forgot, and sometimes, I could even remember the page number and recite the entire passage or chapter of a book.

At the pace I was going, I might be graduating college at eighteen! I do miss my friends from home though, but I love it here!

I often kept in contact with Marco. We would write to each other when I found some down time, and we sometimes talked on the phone, but it seemed that I was always pressed for time and he wasn't.

Marco was in high school now, and he informed me that unfortunately Crystal was now inducted and hanging around with Kelly Mosely and her gang.

She began doing drugs, skipping classes, drinking and getting into trouble. Now, because of Kelly's influence, she was going down the wrong path.

I decided that I had better write to her, hoping I could talk some sense into her, and try again to set things straight between us.

Dear Crystal,

I'm sorry I didn't get a chance to say goodbye to you before I left Bakersfield. I just wanted to tell you that I really liked you, and I hope that you can forgive me for the way I treated you. I was so obsessed with Kelly that I didn't plainly see what a beautiful girl I had right in front of me.

I really care about you, and I don't want you to go down the wrong path.

Marco tells me that you have been associating yourself with Kelly Mosely, and her clan of good for nothings. I am begging you to please stay away from Kelly. There is nothing good that can come from hanging around with her, and I am really worried about you. Please write back to me...I am hoping you will give me a second chance.

Love, Donny

I sent her that letter, and waited with anticipation for many months, hoping for her to reply.

But she never did...I was too late.

Chapter 40

The months began to quickly pass, and soon I was already at the top of my class. I was learning so much about radiation, and its effects on the human body. I was thinking that one day I could actually create a "Hulk" like humanoid with the right combination of chemicals, amino acids and radiation.

Verdi and I are becoming very close, as she literally became my "college mom". She was always watching out for me and feeding me lots of Cuban Empanadas.

Two more years quickly passed, and I was researching and creating phenomenal drugs that the world had never seen before, such as new kinds of natural and synthetic formulations, and I was creating drugs and serums that could someday cure several incurable diseases.

However, I still enjoyed making powerful explosives for fun!

I had engineered a plastic explosive so powerful that a tiny piece, the size of a gum ball could blow the turret off an Army tank! That got snapped up immediately by the Department of Defense and the CIA!

Verdi has been obsessively watching over me, and I never saw, and she never spoke of her husband. The one time I asked her when he was coming back, she said, "Never!" so I left it at that.

I hadn't been home since the day I left, but my parents often drive up to visit me, and they sometimes bring Marco along with them. Seeing Marco brings me back to the old days, and I am reminded of my old neighborhood, Marco, Kelly and Crystal, and even Butt-r-fingers Kenny.

I sometimes wonder what ever happened to Dwain the bus driver, and the rest of the kids that were mean to me. It wasn't fair what I was put through back then just because I was different...In a better way.

I hope someday I could go home and visit the secret waterfall in the woods.

Maybe I could bring Crystal there if she will ever speak to me again.

Chapter 41

One evening during our supper, Verdi informed me that there was going to be a meeting at the Dean's office the following morning.

"Is it about my graduation speech?" I inquired.

"I don't tink so Donny. My boss is calling da meeting, not da Dean," she replied.

"Hmm, I wonder what it's about?" I thought.

I was a little nervous. Maybe I wasn't fulfilling my obligation and they want to kick me out of Caltech and send my dad back to prison!... Naaa, that couldn't be it.

I guess I'll find out tomorrow what they want.

Early the following morning we met outside the Dean's office in a small waiting room.

Three large gentlemen wearing black suits were sitting there, chain smoking cigarettes.

"Are you guys going to a funeral?" I joked.

The men just sat there, and continued puffing away, and didn't respond.

"I can tell you guys that someday "the cat will be out of the bag," and it will be revealed that the nicotine in those cigarettes is addictive. The tobacco companies are spending millions covering that up.

All those nasty carcinogens from the smoke will definitely catch up to you later on, and you'll probably die of lung cancer if you don't stop smoking right now," I stated.

The men just ignored me, and continued smoking. Verdi nudged me, and told me to be quiet. She whispered that these men were from the FBI, CIA and the Justice Department.

Suddenly the Dean's door opened, and Senator Blackstone came out with the Dean.

"Donny, so nice to see you again!" he exclaimed.

I stood up, and we firmly shook hands. Something Verdi taught me. A simple handshake can send a powerful message about a person's character. I want the Senator to know that I'm not a kid anymore.

"I understand you are doing some phenomenal things here at Caltech. I knew you were going to do great things if you had the right resources and environment," declared the Senator.

"Thank you Senator. If it wasn't for you, I'd still be stuck at my old school and blowing up pumpkins in my backyard," I replied.

Senator Blackstone then turned to the Dean and thanked him for the use of his office.

"Unfortunately we have some Top Secret issues to discuss, and you don't have a security clearance Dean, so you'll have to leave. There are no listening devices in your office are there?" the Senator half heartedly joked.

The Dean laughed, and gathered a few stacks of papers while leaving.

"Actually just the intercom to my secretary, but she's not a Communist," he joked as he walked out of the office.

"Hello Donny, just don't put your feet up on my desk, okay!" chuckled the Dean .

"Come in lady and Gentleman," the Senator stated. Verdi prompted me to enter the office, as the Senator was unplugging the intercom.

The three men in black also arose, and followed Verdi and I into the office. I noticed one of the men had a peculiar limp. The Senator sat in the Dean's hefty leather swivel chair that was stationed behind his large walnut desk. We sat down in front of the Senator in the 5 empty chairs that were placed there.

"Good morning Gentlemen, 'This is Donny Lord'. Donny, these men are from some very important governmental agencies. Their names are not important but they are here to meet you and talk to you about something they have on their minds.

Remember back when I was sitting at your kitchen table, and I told you that we will be expecting you to start working for the government?" stated the Senator.

I began to get a little worried because these men were staring at me intensely. I couldn't imagine what they had in store for me.

One of the men stood up, and introduced himself.

"Good Morning Donny, my name is 'Mr. None Of Your Business'. The man sitting next to me is 'Mr. Nobody,' and the other gentleman here is 'Mr. What's It To Ya,'" he discreetly stated.

"Wait a minute.... I just want to get this straight...The guy with the limp, he's 'Mr. Nobody'. The other guy is 'Mr. What's It To Ya,' and you are 'Mr. None Of Your Business?'" I chuckled.

Verdi gave me a stern look to stop messing with these men.

"That's right, in other words our names are Top Secret, and as far as you're concerned we don't exist.

So Donny, let's just get right into the tip of the horn of why we are all here.

We know about the serum you produced back in your basement that caused your neighbors dog to age abruptly. We are very interested in that serum, and we need you to go full in, and begin working on it again. We need you to perfect it, polish it, and get it working in a safe and permanent manner," stated Mr. None Of Your Business.

I sat there puzzled and confused.

"Why would anyone want a serum that would increase the age of animals? If anything, shouldn't we be trying to help animals stay youthful and to help them live longer? That psychotic dog aged a large number of years in just a few hours, and then he died prematurely!" I proclaimed.

"First of all, you are not in a position to ask who, what, why or whatever. All you need to know is that we need you to make the serum, and you will do what we ask, or all of this will come crashing down on you, kid!" threatened Mr. None Of Your Business.

The Senator quickly jumped in, and diffused the situation.

"Okay, okay, let's settle down here Mr. None Of Your Business, there is no need to push him," stated the Senator

"Donny, these gentlemen don't have the patience and grace you and I have, since they are not used to anyone pushing them back. What we are just asking for you to do is just get back to the ageing serum, and see what kind of progress you can make in the next few months," stated the Senator.

"Does this have something to do with 'The Silver Orchid?'" I asked.

Upon hearing me say "The Silver Orchid" the three gentlemen angrily jumped up, and began yelling at me!

"How do you know about 'The Silver Orchid!'

That is Top Secret information!!" Mr. None Of Your Business shouted.

"I tol him," confessed Verdi.

"After I killed da Russians dat was chasing us, he asked me why dey were after him. I didn't tink it was a big deal to tell him, and he had da right to know," she stated.

"You didn't "tink" it was a big deal! You do not have the authority to make those decisions you stupid Cuban bitch!" Mr. Nobody angrily shouted.

Verdi instantly lost her violent temper and lunged at him! She began wildly punching him in the face and kicking him with her knee incessantly!!

"What ju say to me ju piece a chit!! I kill you!!" she screamed.

Mr. What's It To You, and Mr. None Of Your Business were desperately trying to stop her violent rage, and they finally managed to pull her off him! Mr. Nobody tried to pull himself together as he quickly stumbled and staggered out of the office, bleeding and shouting "She's crazy!!".

We all stood there looking at each other as Verdi calmly sat back down in her chair, and removed a small compact mirror from her purse and daintily began tidying up her makeup and hair without saying a word.

"Well Donny, since you already know. Yes this is what we are referring to as 'The Silver Orchid'. That's all we can tell you about it right now, but we would appreciate it if you kept it under wraps for the time being," stated the Senator.

"I understand, and I'll do my best. I just need a little time to review my notes and draw out the molecular chains to see how the hormones, nucleic and amino acids, and the ionic and polar bonds interacted to cause that aging process," I stated.

"Whatever you say kid, do whatever you have to do," laughed the Senator.

The two remaining men abruptly stood up and pulled cigarette boxes from their shirt pockets and left the room.

"Uhh just one more thing Senator," I said.

"Yes Donny?" I was wondering when I would be getting that car you promised me? It would really make me happy and really boost my creative juices ya know?" I joked.

"Fair enough Donny, fair enough," the Senator chuckled.

Verdi and I stood up and we shook the Senators hand and we left the office.

"Geez Verdi, what the hell happened in there?!!" I exclaimed.

"Dat scumbag, he waz my boss, and my lover. Dat piece a chit is still in love wid me, but he had a wife and kids he never tell me about. When I find out he was a married guy wid kidz, I get so angry, I tried to castrate him," she matter of factly stated.

"So what happened?!" I asked.

"I missed, dats why he walk so funny!" she laughed.

We walked together, back to our apartment, and I asked her about her husband.

"Dat was a bull chit story dey tol ju. Dey first thought maybe dey needed two agents to protect ju but den dey call Verdi to da job. I never had a husband. "I don't need no man," she smugly stated.

Chapter 42

When we arrived back at the apartment, I immediately began looking through my old boxes of notebooks and files from home, until I found the one with the "Muscleman serum" in it.

It was funny for me to look back at my old notes. Just as a high school senior might look back and find his first grade homework hidden in a long lost box and wonder how first grade seemed so difficult at the time. I see and understand everything so much clearer now.

Within a few hours I had an understanding of the process of how the molecular chains were creating rapid aging, but I was still missing a few important factors relating to its side effects.

I had the serum somewhat close when I injected it into Chomper. When I injected the rat at the science fair, adding Geritol only made matters worse because it converted some of the enzymes into hydrogen gas, thus inflating the rat, and making it float like the Hindenburg blimp before it exploded.

After a few weeks of reconfiguring the chemical, and molecular bonds I was very close to perfecting "The Silver Orchid".

Depending on how much serum I injected into a rat, would determine how many years the rat would age.

For example, 1cc of serum would equal 10 years of aging, and 5 cc would equate to 50 years and so on.

It was working perfectly on rats and other small rodents. When I then branched out testing the serum on small monkeys, cats, dogs and even chimps. The test subjects weight had no inference relating to the amount of serum required. Each subject depending on the serum dosage seemed to age proportionally in a matter of hours!

It was staggering to watch a vibrant young chimp age 30 years sometimes in an hour!

First it's hair would turn silver and then some teeth would start to discolor and fall out. The skin would become limp and wrinkly and typically warts or boils would begin to form. The body would become atrophied and mobility declined depending on how much serum I injected. It was just as if they were aging naturally but in only a few minutes.

The only common side effect that I noticed in all the test subjects was a faint reddish secretion coming from their tear ducts. It was difficult to see unless it was hit just right by the sunlight, and if you knew to look for it.

I still couldn't understand why the government wanted a serum to age animals. Maybe it was some form of pest control or a way to mature farm animals to slaughter more efficiently.

I arrived home one evening after spending all day at school, and I noticed Verdi on the phone. She began whispering when she noticed that I came into the apartment. She was watching me, and kept turning her back to me when I passed by. Finally she hung up the phone.

"What was that all about?" I questioned.

"De Senator, he anxious to know how ju are making out with da Silver Orchid," she replied.

"So what did you tell him?" I asked.

"I tol him to come see for himself. He is coming here tomorrow. Ju ready?" she asked.

"Yeah, I'm ready," I confidently replied.

"I hope he brings me that car tomorrow!" I stated.

Chapter 43

I was preparing an injection of the Silver Orchid serum, when the Senator arrived at my laboratory the following morning, followed by the same three men in black.

"Well if it isn't Mr. None Of Your Business, Mr. What's It To Ya, and Mr. Nobody," I smugly joked.

The three men wearing their classic black suits and dark sunglasses emotionlessly nodded at me as they entered the lab.

Verdi just coldly stared at Mr. Nobody,

"Mang, why ju walk so funny?" she chuckled.

He became angry and insisted that she had to leave the room.

The Senator looked at her, and nodded his head toward the door. She smirked, and coolly strutted out of the room, blowing Mr. Nobody a kiss as she slowly closed the door behind her. I directed the men to gather around my large slate lab table.

"Donny, we are really excited to be here today to see what progress you have made with the Silver Orchid." stated the Senator.

I turned off the lights, and started a projector slide show onto a large white screen.

"Please observe the chronological chain of events on these test specimens," I stated.

I projected several time lapsed photographs of different rodents aging at calibrated intervals. I also displayed several cats, dogs and primates.

"As you can observe, each participant transformed from a normal healthy young specimen, to an advanced, debilitated geriatric specimen in a matter of minutes to an hour. Based on the amount of 'The Silver Orchid' injected, determined the amount of time the specimen progressed. The only harmless side effect is a slight change to their tear ducts. Instead of clear tears they are producing a tear with a slight reddish tint to it," I explained

I turned the lights back on, and the men seemed skeptical.

"That's impossible! The kid used different animals at different ages and doctored the slides to look like they were aging!" shouted Mr. Nobody.

"Ya know Mr. No-booty, an accusation like that really hurts my feelings," I sarcastically stated.

I then removed an infant kitten from a cage and injected it with the serum. In a matter of minutes it began to increase in size and grew up to the size of a full grown pussy cat!

The men were totally astonished and could not believe their eyes!

"Well done Donny!" stated the Senator as he applauded my work.

The three "G" men quickly left the Lab, and raced out of the building toward a batch of pay phone booths that were stationed outside.

They were frantically searching for coins, and began chattering away in an extremely excited manner.

"So did I do good?" I asked the Senator.

"Spectacular job Kid! Now here's what's going to happen. We're going to have to take this show on the road, and prove that it works for a few of the higher, higher ups. Can you whip up a batch of 'The Orchid' and be ready for a live presentation for tomorrow?" the Senator asked.

"Yes sir, I have plenty already made," I replied.

"Good, then bring enough to age a bull. And bring the formula outline. I'll pick you up tomorrow at 9 AM," he stated.

"Pick me up? It's not going to be here in my lab?" I questioned.

"No, it's going to be at a restricted location, you don't get car sick do you kid?" he joked.

"No, but if I did, I'd make sure to invent a pill to prevent it...I might call it Don-a-mine," I jokingly replied.

The Senator laughed, and started toward the door.

"I'll see you tomorrow Donny. Tell Verdi to be ready, she should be there too. Oh, I almost forgot something!" he exclaimed.

The Senator stopped and searched through several of his jacket pockets. He then tossed a jingly object toward me and I caught it. I looked down into my hand and it was a set of keys attached to a Corvette emblemed key chain!

"It's parked in a secure secret garage on campus. Verdi will take you there. See you tomorrow kid, and again great work, I'm really proud of you!" stated the Senator.

Verdi came strolling back into the room as the Senator quickly walked out.

"So, ju want to see jur car, or do ju want to play with jur mice?" she joked.

"Yahoo! Lets go!" I shouted.

She took me to a location on the opposite end of campus. There was a concrete ramp which led down into an inconspicuous abandoned tunnel. A heavy iron gate securing it's entrance was concealed by a dense layer of thick Ivy. She put a key into a hidden slot and the gate began to rise. As the gate went up, I could see the glint of the bright shiny chrome bumper of my new red corvette!

"Are we in the Bat cave, Robin!?" I joked.

I ran over and jumped into the car! Carefully I placed the key into the ignition. Ahhh, the sweet smell of "new car" was heavy in the air! I turned the key and the beast came alive!

I carefully drove out of the garage, and we took a drive up to the mountains. It was so much fun! Up and down and around the mountain roads!

I couldn't wait to call Marco, and tell him all about it! We spent the whole day out, just driving around the back roads and up in the mountains, but eventually we had to go home.

Chapter 44

Early the following morning a long black limousine was waiting outside of our building for us. I gathered my supplies, and placed them in a small doctor style bag and off we went.

We drove about two hours when we finally entered a highly restricted governmental complex in the middle of nowhere. We were directed to a large contemporary building, and when we entered it, we were given High Security ID badges.

I followed Verdi, since she seemed to know where we were supposed to go, and we finally ended up taking an elevator down about 50 feet into the basement.

"Verdi, did I ever tell you the story about how when I was a kid, my father freaked out in an elevator at a department store when the doors wouldn't open?" I chuckled.

She just smiled, and stared at the numbers declining above the elevator door.

When the elevator finally stopped, there was a very long pause as we waited for the door to slide open.

"Gee, I didn't think that door was ever going to open, and I almost freaked out too!" I joked.

I continued following Verdi down a long hallway, and we entered a large room that had a wet unpainted concrete floor. There were floor drains incrementally spaced across the floor and I noticed some red blood stains on the cement.

It reminded me of the kill room floor at the meat packing plant, where they had just hosed all the animal blood off the floor and washed it down the drain.

The room contained all sorts of incline tables with arm and leg restraints. Some were positioned over water tubs, and there were several maniacal "electric chairs" with restraining straps and gags that seemed to be archaic torture devices.

"What the hell is this place?" I frightfully asked.

"Dis is da CIA interrogation room. No try to be funny here. Deez guyz are crazy son um a bitches, and dey don't like jokes," she whispered.

Just then a small army of men and women in white lab coats, and several security guards entered the room. The Senator, None Of Your Business, What's It To Ya, and Mr. Nobody were leading the pack.

"Hello Donny, how do you like your new Corvette?!" gleamed the Senator.

"Thank you so much. That car Senator, it's so cool!" I exclaimed.

"So Donny, you must be wondering why we've brought you down here. You've been doing such a great job for us, but we need to bring "The Silver Orchid" up to the next level," he stated.

"I am sort of wondering, why are you so interested in aging animals," I replied.

"Well you are going to find out today, son," replied the Senator.

Mr. None Of Your Business motioned to the guards, and they quickly left the room.

It was quiet and we stood around awkwardly for a few minutes, until we heard off in the distance an iron door unlock, clank open and then slam shut.

Then we heard a tumult coming from down the hallway toward us. We heard a man screaming and shouting all sorts of obscenities, presumably at the guards as he was resisting them.

The ruckus became louder and louder as the guards moved down the hallway towards us, obviously struggling with the man they were escorting! They finally burst into the room dragging an extremely resistant shackled prisoner with them. They aggressively threw him on a table, and strapped him down!

I stood there in shock since I had never seen anything like this happen before! The restrained man continued shouting obscenities at the men until they finally gagged him with a leather mask.

"Donny, this creature is a convicted quintuple murderer. His name is Paul Patterson. About 5 years ago, he strangled his pregnant wife and stabbed his three small children thirty times each! He then drank their blood and mutilated their bodies and then dumped them into a garbage dumpster behind the kids school! He wanted to get rid of his entire family so that he could carry on with another woman he had just met while working at the post office.

Maybe you had heard about it on the news? They called him "Count Post-ula" and he's where the term "Going Postal" was derived from.

He evaded the death penalty on a minor legal technicality and instead of being put to death he was given a "life" sentence.

A lot of people in high places were very upset that he got to live after what he had done to his pregnant wife, the baby who was in the third trimester of her pregnancy, and those poor little innocent children.

We'd like you to inject this remorseless, maniacal murderer with your serum to see if we can speed things up a bit, and 'legitimately' shorten his time on earth. This way we won't have to waste taxpayer money taking care of this piece of garbage for the rest of his life, and in the end, he'll get what's duly coming to him," stated the Senator.

"Wait a minute Senator! I was under the impression that this was for animal use! I never intended this to be used on humans! I don't know if it will even work, and it might kill him!" I exclaimed.

"Don't worry about that Donny, this is all for the sake of science," replied the Senator.

"Come on kid, let's get to it!" shouted Mr. None Of Your Business.

Everyone closed in around the table to observe the injection take place, and there were also two gentlemen filming the procedure.

"Well how old is he? I nervously asked.

"He is 32 years old, and weighs 193 pounds," stated one of the white coats.

"The weight doesn't matter. How many years do you want to add on to him?" I asked.

"Let's start out with 55 years that would take him to 87 years old," stated Mr. None Of Your Business.

I drew 5.5cc's into a large syringe, and approached the man.

I began getting nervous about sticking a needle into a human, despite how terrible of a person he was.

"Okay everyone...I made this stuff, but I am not going to be the one that injects it into him!" I firmly stated.

The Senator nodded to one of the white coats who appeared to be a doctor, and he took the syringe from me. He asked me if it was to be injected muscular or intravenous. I told him to inject it into the man's jugular vein for a quicker response, and I pointed to the area on the man's neck.

"Thanks, but I do know where the jugular is kid," the doctor sarcastically stated.

The prisoner began violently fighting and screaming when he saw the needle and heard what was about to take place! A few of the guards held his head steady as the white coat doctor inserted the needle into his neck and injected the serum. After about 15 seconds he calmed down, and stopped fighting.

I was contemplating that maybe the serum wouldn't work, since I never experimented with it on a human before. Suddenly the man began having convulsions and his restrained body began shaking violently out of control.

"Oh boy! I don't think this is going to be pretty," I exclaimed.

Suddenly the man just stiffly arched his back and passed out. A guard then removed the leather gag from the prisoners face.

Then, after a short pause, the man's hair began turning gray, and his skin was loosening and becoming wrinkly. I noticed his eyes were slightly discharging a reddish fluid, which I pointed out to the individuals in the room.

"That's the tell tale side effect of the serum," I stated.

We stayed there and watched minute by minute as he was transforming into an old man. After about 30 minutes, the transformation seemed to be complete and he awoke.

He was then unbuckled, and the security guards lifted him to his feet.

"What the hell did you son of a bitches do to me?!!" he moaned as his teeth were falling out of his mouth onto the floor!

They easily dragged the "old man" over to a mirror, and when he saw himself, he began shrieking in horror!

"What have you done to me!! Who's that old man in the mirror!! I'm in the Twilight zone!!" he screamed.

"Get him out of here!" shouted Mr. None Of Your Business.

The guards then dragged him out of the room as he was still shouting and cursing, and they quickly left dragging him down the hallway.

The room was totally silent, when suddenly the whole group that was assembled there, including Verdi began to loudly cheer and applaud!

"You did it kid!!" the Senator shouted as he hugged me, and shook me in delight!

I have to say, that even though it was a really heinous thing to do, it felt pretty good getting such great accolades from the crew!

The people began swiftly leaving the room, chattering about what they had just witnessed. One of white coats approached me and took the vial containing the serum out of my bag. He stated that they were going to need the formula as well. I was extremely apprehensive when I saw my serum leaving the room without me.

When the Senator saw that I was going to object, he reminded me…

"Donny, remember, everything you create becomes the property of the US government".

I reluctantly nodded and backed off. I reached into my shirt pocket and handed the formula over to the Senator.

"Thank you Donny, I just want you to understand that we will not be using your serum to hurt innocent people, just the bad ones.

Our prisons are so overcrowded, and we were reasoning how productive it would be if someone could just serve time without doing the time. Sitting in jail waiting for years to pass while occupying space with full room and board is a great expense. Not to mention full medical and dental benefits. Imprisonment is a huge expense to the government. The money saved could go to benefit our law abiding citizens, rather than be wasted on criminals.

Now, thanks to you, we can literally just take 5, 10, 20 or more years off a criminal's life without them having to do the time!

Of course there will be exceptions. Violent criminals would still be incarcerated to protect the public, and some will be put to death, but the government will save billions of dollars!" exclaimed the Senator.

"Let me get this straight. My serum will keep people out of prison but their bodies will degenerate and age as if their time was actually spent in prison?" I questioned.

"Genius isn't it!" exclaimed the Senator.

"I remembered there was once a time when my father was in prison. I was thinking about what a waste of time it was to be locked up, and the years of your precious life wiped away by the time you finally get out. I'm not so sure if this is a good thing, but it seems to make sense," I stated.

"Thank you Donny, now get back to your lab, and keep up the good work. Maybe another great break through like the 'DLSO'" gloated the Senator.

"Uhhm..'DLSO' sir?" I questioned.

"It's the acronym we came up with for the Silver Orchid.

It stands for 'Donny Lord's Silver Orchid'. We felt you created it, so you should get the glory.

"Gee thanks...I guess I'm flattered," I sarcastically replied.

"By the way son, Mr. Nobody needs a drug to initiate terrorists to quickly speak up and not withhold information. The serum they are using now is old and outdated.

The detainees are still able to lie. Can you start working on that too?" the Senator questioned.

"I'm on it sir…The only problem is, how am I going to interrogate a mouse to identify if it's withholding information on the whereabouts that it may have hid its cheese?" I joked.

"I'm sure you'll figure something out," replied the Senator.

The ride home was awkward. Verdi and I quietly sat in the back of the limo, and I couldn't get the image of that guy flopping around, strapped down on that table out of my head.

"That was pretty wild, huh Verdi?" I asked.

"Donny, Ju one smart dude to make dat chit," she stated.

"Jes, I am," I smugly replied.

Chapter 45

As time passed, I continued on with my research, and worked diligently for the government as well as discovering new treatments and medicines for many diseases and disorders.

I lived in my laboratory. Not because I was forced to, but because it was the only place I felt comfortable and at home. I never had much time for girls, and on the few occasions when I did have dates, it was awkward with Verdi lurking in the shadows behind us.

I had almost forgotten about the Silver Orchid until one afternoon, I noticed a custodian who I hadn't seen for a few months. He was back at work, and looked noticeably aged.

"Excuse me sir, but are you okay? The last time I saw you, you appeared about 20 years younger," I simply stated.

The man glanced at me, and I could see in his eyes the tell tale sign of a slight reddish tint, that I had seen many times before.

The man became nervous, and turned away.

"You don't know me from shit!" he stated, and he continued cleaning.

"My god, they are actually implementing 'The Silver Orchid' for real," I thought in dire amazement.

After that day, I noticed that it was becoming more and more apparent, and prevalent to encounter people all around me, who were seemingly "aged". The eerie part of it was walking down the street, and staring into all these elderly criminal soles with the reddish wash in their eyes.

Whenever I saw them, I knew exactly who they were.

It was my doing. My serum did this to them.

Chapter 46

It was my 21st birthday, and my parents came up to school to visit me. It's been 5 years since I left home. It was really great to see them, and Marco also came along.

Marco has been working with his father since he graduated High school. It is a little vague what he actually does, but he seems to be doing something involved with his father's collections and insurance.

He claims he's a "leg breaker," but I think maybe he is kidding.

Marco had asked me if he could see my lab so I took him for a tour while my parents sat and chatted with Verdi.

"Wow this place is really cool!" he said.

"Yep, this is where I do all my work," I replied.

"Hey Donny, do you think you can whip me up a batch of Spanish Fly?" he half heartedly joked.

"Man, I can make you some serious fly, my friend! As a matter of fact, I'll make you something even better, a really potent Italian fly!

All you'll have to do is drink my potion and the girls will be going nuts over you!" I convincingly stated.

His eyes lit up, and he suddenly became interested in what science could do for him. Some people never change.

"Okay, but can you hurry up before your parents come walking in here!" he exclaimed.

I grabbed a beaker, and began mixing "a little bit of this, and a little bit of that" until the liquid began bubbling and smoking in the beaker as it turned into a dark brown elixir.

"Okay drink this concoction, and you will be the desire of every hot woman who makes eye contact with you! Beware though, do not make eye contact with anyone you don't want!" I exclaimed.

He eagerly grabbed the beaker, and without any hesitation, began gulping down the liquid until the beaker was empty.

"Hey this tastes like a cherry cola ice cream soda!" he exclaimed.

It tasted that way because it was an artificially flavored cherry cola ice cream soda! I invented several artificial flavors, and I just wanted to see if it would pass Marco's discriminate taste test.

I think for fun, I'll just let him go on thinking he drank the "Italian fly" potion.

"When is this stuff going to kick in?!!" he anxiously questioned.

"Ohhh… very soon, and then "Watch Out!" you will be overrun by hot horny women! Just remember what I told you about the eye contact thing. If I were you I wouldn't look anyone in the eyes that you don't want to fall in love with you," I chuckled.

It was easier just to let him go on thinking he had now achieved some magical powers, than to disappoint him.

"Hey, I just remembered that I wanted to tell you something!" exclaimed Marco.

"I saw Kelly Mosely and Crystal about a month ago. They were both at the courthouse. I was there waiting on one of my dad's clients to post bail when I saw them huddled in a corner. I don't know what happened to them but they looked like old Hags!" he sadly stated.

"Old Hags? Like how old?" I was concerned.

"Well, Kelly looked as if she was sixty years old, and Crystal looked to be like fortyish! I think it's the drugs, and the booze. Kelly has been a heroin junkie ever since high school. Crystal has stayed clean but is still sort of hanging out with her. Maybe more so to help her get straightened out. Based on how she looked, she must be into something though," stated Marco.

"You don't know if they ever got in trouble with the police, do you?" I fearfully asked.

"Funny thing, I heard they both got busted about a year ago. Crystal picked up Kelly one day, and they went to Burger King for something to eat. Crystal wanted to take Kelly out and buy her some food, since she never eats much on account of her drug habit. The parking lot was jammed up with high school kids, and there were no parking spots. Kelly insisted she would go in and get the food while Crystal waited out in the car. So Crystal gave Kelly the money, and Kelly went inside to get the food to go.

Kelly goes in, and orders the food, and when she gets the bag of burgers, instead of handing over the money, she pulls out a knife from the back of her shorts, and robs the Burger king!

She hustled back into the car, and Crystal not knowing what Kelly had done, drove off.

Two minutes later, the cops surrounded their car and they both got busted. They claimed Crystal was an accomplice even though Kelly admitted Crystal didn't have anything to do with it," stated Marco.

"I know Crystal's father is a high powered attorney, maybe he got them off?" I replied.

"I doubt it, I mean armed robbery is a pretty serious offence just to get off scot free," stated Marco.

"Does Crystal and Kelly still live at home?" I asked.

"I don't think so. Both of their parents got fed up, and kicked them out to the curb. I think Crystal now works at the Pizza House, to make ends meet," Marco stated.

"Come on...let's get out of here and get back to my party. By the way Marco, for some reason I feel like I want to make out with you!" I joked.

"Yeah, I can't wait to see if this "Italian fly" stuff is going to work!" exclaimed Marco.

It was hilarious watching Marco avoiding eye contact with my mother, but struggling to get Verdi's attention and to get her to "look into his eyes!".

<h1 style="text-align:center">Chapter 47</h1>

I couldn't stop thinking about Crystal and Kelly. How things could have been so much different if only I had the nerve to knock on Kelly's door after that day at the waterfall. Kelly wouldn't be on drugs. Crystal would probably be in law school, and it was all my stupid fault!

It bothered me for days, and finally one morning I told Verdi that I needed to take a trip back home, and I was either going with her or without her.

"Ju not going anywhere wid out me, Kid," she firmly stated.

"Well let's go get the Corvette, we are taking a road trip to Bakersfield," I stated.

"Why we are going der?" she inquired.

"I'm on a rescue mission," I replied.

We were soon on our way, and the closer we got to home, the more familiar things became to me. I hadn't been back to my hometown for so long. Everything had changed.

When we finally exited the highway and rolled up to a stop light, I noticed the streets were crowded with people walking and shopping. Oddly, there were so many "old" people strolling around. I couldn't tell if it was because of my serum, or if they were just old people.

As I drove down Main Street, I happened to recognize a few of the kids from my old high school. They were staring at me as I drove by in my Corvette.

"That's right losers, it's me, the Science Nerd Donny Lord!" I felt like shouting.

"Do you feel like a pizza Verdi?" I asked.

"I don't care, go where ever ju want, as long as I can smoke my Chigar," she stated.

I parked my car outside the Pizza House where Crystal and I had our first date. I was so nervous about going in, but I hoped that Marco was correct and Crystal was still working there.

The restaurant was almost empty when we entered.

Verdi did a visual surveillance scan of the restaurant for potential risks, then went straight to the ladies room. I sat down at the table next to the front window where Crystal and I had once sat together. I saw the back of a tall slender redheaded waitress wearing faded bell bottom blue jeans and an untucked green plaid flannel shirt. She was cleaning the menu board when she suddenly realized someone had come in behind her, and had sat down at a table.

My heart began to pound as I waited for her to turn around. I picked up a menu, and hid my face so as not to be immediately recognized. I heard her notice my presence, and she walked over with a small green pad and pen to take my order.

"Hi, I'm Crystal, what can I get for you?" she sweetly asked. I recognized her voice immediately.

"Hi Crystal…do you remember me?" I softly asked, as I put the menu down, and stood up.

She was shocked and stunned, as if she had just seen a ghost, and began backing away from me. I immediately noticed the red blush in her eyes, and her aged complexion. She had definitely been injected with the Silver Orchid, but she was still beautiful despite that. Crystal blossomed from that geeky girl in high school to a gorgeous red headed beauty like her mother.

"Well, if it isn't Donny freaking Lord," she scowled.

"I'm sorry, I didn't mean to scare you, I know it's been awhile Crystal," I quietly stated.

"What the hell are you doing here? Shouldn't you be book worming it back at Caltech with your sorority girl friends?" she scolded.

"Crystal, I came back here to see you, and to talk to you, and to hopefully get some answers. But first I want to tell you that the morning after our date, I went to your house to see you, and to apologize for the way I treated you. You weren't there, but your mother and maid gave me a real hard time. I insisted that I really needed to talk to you, but your mother wouldn't have any part of it and told me to get lost, and then she slammed the door in my face. I sent you a letter which you never responded to. Then Marco told me you started hanging around with Kelly," I stated.

"I never got your letter, and I never heard that you came over to my house. I'm sure my mother had everything to do with keeping that from me," she angrily replied.

"But I had sent you letters too, and you never responded back to me either," she insisted.

I was instantly taken aback by her statement!

"I never got any letters! I swear!" I exclaimed.

I saw Verdi coming out of the restroom, and I motioned to her not to come over, so she sat down at another table and looked at a menu while glancing over at us.

"What did your letter say, Donny? That you were a jerk and you really hurt me?" she exclaimed.

"I was afraid that if you started hanging around with Kelly and her crew, that you would turn out like her, and I wanted to stop you. I also wrote that I wanted another chance for us," I sincerely stated.

"Well Donny, do ya really want to know why I started hanging around with Kelly, and her loser friends? Because I wanted you to like me! Whatever you saw in her, I wanted it! There was something about her that you were obsessed with! For the way she treated you, and the fact that you were still in love with her, I just thought either you were a glutton for punishment, or you were attracted to mean girls.

I just wanted you to like me, and it was obvious that you didn't like 'nerd' Crystal, so I tried to change into 'bitch' Kelly! Don't you really want a bad girl, Donny!" she shouted.

"No Crystal, I liked you the way you were! And it wasn't because Kelly was mean and rotten that I liked her. It was because of our time together before that. We were very close when we were kids, and I was holding on to some of those emotional memories. Now, I'm back to try to fix the things I messed up!" I exclaimed.

Crystal softened her stance, but avoided making eye contact and she kept turning away from me in an effort to hide her aged complexion.

"What did your letters say Crystal?" I questioned.

"That I loved you, and that I wanted to be with you!" she teared up and began crying.

My whole life seemed to be a tragic tumult of missed opportunities, and screw ups! I thought to myself.

"What's Kelly doing now?" I asked.

"After what happened at the Burger king, I stopped trying to help her. Now we are both old and ugly because she got me mixed up into something I had nothing to do with. My parents kicked me out of the house, and refused to pay for my college," she cried.

"I don't think you are ugly, in fact, I think you are very beautiful," I softly stated.

"You think I'm beautiful, looking like this?" she blushed.

"Yes, and now I'm here to help you. I know you and Kelly were injected with the Silver Orchid," I said.

"Silver Orchid, what's that?" she questioned.

"DLSO is probably what they are calling it," I whispered.

Her eyes widened, and she was taken aback.

"How do you know about that?!" she exclaimed.

"I know about it because I'm the one who invented it," I remorsefully stated.

She became complacent, and looked as if she was going to faint, and we sat down at my table.

"When they injected us, we had to sign confidentiality agreements not to talk, or tell anyone about it, or we would get thrown into prison," she reported.

"How much of a dose did you get, and how much did Kelly get?" I questioned.

"I got 20 years and Kelly got 40 years," she somberly stated, as her eyes gazed down at the floor.

"Where is Kelly now?" I asked.

"Kelly is still with Kenny. They are both strung out heroin addicts, and they live in a crack house across town. Kenny has gotten at least 3 DLSO injections equaling about 60 years," she replied.

"Crystal, I'm so happy to see you, but I have to leave now. I will be back as soon as I can figure things out. I really need to know how to get in touch with you, okay?" I insisted.

She eagerly wrote her address, and phone number on an order slip, and passed it to me.

"I'll be in touch with you in a few weeks. I promise," I firmly stated, and I embraced her goodbye.

I motioned to Verdi that we were leaving, and she followed me out the door.

"Hey what about dat pizza?" she complained.

"Come on, let's go. The pizza here is overrated," I replied.

We got back into my car, and I noticed Crystal watching me from the restaurant window, and she waved to me as I left.

As we drove off I began telling Verdi the story of Crystal and Kelly.

"I don't get something Verdi. We both sent each other letters, but neither of us got them. I'm sure her mother intercepted my letter but why didn't I get hers?" I questioned.

She sat there silently, and I noticed that she was uncomfortable.

"Verdi, do you know anything about those letters?" I demanded.

She took a deep breath, then fell on the sword.

"Kid, when we first getting started, my boss 'Mr. Nobody' had guys checking your mail. Dey don't want ju distracted, and maybe sending secrets to da girl. Dey don't want nobody knowing where ju lived except jur friend Marco and jur parents.

Da girl she just send da letters to Caltech wid no address, but dey know how to get dem to ju. Dey jus trew dem in da garbage," she reluctantly stated.

"Dammit!!" I shouted. As I smashed my hands against the steering wheel!

But in hindsight, I could have done more to get in touch with Crystal too. I could have had Marco talk to her for me. I guess at the time I was just too obsessed with my work.

"It's Okay Verdi, everything happens for a reason, I suppose".

Chapter 48

When I arrived back at school, I began sifting through my notes. There must be a way to reverse the Silver Orchid, and I have to figure it out.

I worked many days and nights on reversing the molecular chains and amino acid combinations. It was more complicated than I could ever imagine. Basically I was trying to discover the fountain of youth.

Finally after a few weeks, I began to understand a possible way to reverse the serum. However, it would entail using a rare radioactive isotope to excite the atoms to revert back to the way they once were.

The cure could potentially be worse than the elderly state they were in.

There was also a good possibility of severe side effects such as radiation poisoning, cancer or even instantaneous death. I needed to find a radioactive element that had a very short half life. I thought about it for a few minutes, and suddenly it hit me! "The element Astatine {At} 85!" A derivative of Francium. I believe the half life is only a few hours, and it might just be enough to get the molecules to revert!

But Astatine is so rare that it really doesn't exist, unless I can isolate it from breaking down the atoms of Francium. Given that, I won't have much time to utilize the atoms before they begin degenerating. My guess, I'll have about 6 or 8 hours max.

The big problem is, I don't have any heavy elements, let alone any Francium. I'll have to go see what they have stored in the main science building. There must be something in there that I can use.

The following morning, I rushed over to the science center, and knocked on Professor Prygocci's door.

"Get lost Lord!" I heard from the other side of the thick wooden door.

"Professor Prygocci, please I need to speak to you!" I shouted through the closed door.

"What part of "get lost" don't you understand, rectum?!" he cursed.

"I need to talk to you about a project I'm working on, and I need your help," I shouted through the door.

Suddenly I heard the wheels of a chair squeak and roll, and the door unlocked and swung open!

"The Golden Tool needs my help?! For years you made me look like a total jackass in front of my students and colleagues! Always contradicting me, and constantly proving me wrong! They retracted my PhD because of you, and now you need "MY" help?!" he shouted.

"Well yes, yes I do," I replied.

"Go ahead, enlighten me, turd breath. What can I do for the great Donny Lord," he sarcastically stated.

"I need some Uraninite mineral ASAP," I simply stated.

The professor looked at me cross eyed, then burst out laughing.

"Are you crazy! That shit is under complete lock down in the radiation lab, and by the way, go to hell!

We only have a 55 gram piece of it, and it's one of the only pieces in the whole USA!

It's worth a fortune, and I hate to burst the bubble of the great Donny Lord, but it's MINE, and I need it for MY work that I'm doing to try to regain my PhD!" he exclaimed.

I walked right past him and barged into his office. Among the tall piles of uncorrected papers, and old scientific magazines scattered about on his messy desk, I found the telephone.

"May I use your phone?" I politely asked.

"Go ahead puke breath, but you'll never get my Uraninite!" he scowled.

I dialed the number, and waited as the phone rang. The professor casually sat back down in his chair, and wheeled himself back to his desk. He began doodling scary decapitated doll images on a piece of paper, and began gibbering to himself.

"I'll throw that rock in the ocean before I let this dip shit have it," he smugly mumbled to himself.

Just then the phone was answered.

"Senator Blackstone here," was the response.

"Hi Senator, this is Donny Lord".

"Hello Donny, how are you doing?" replied the Senator.

"Well not so good. I'm not happy Senator. I'm working on something big, and I need a mineral sample that Professor Prygocci has locked up, and he is refusing to give it to me. Not only that, but he is threatening to toss it into the ocean rather than let me have it," I stated.

"Okay Donny, I understand," and he hung up the phone.

"I guess you're out of luck ya dilwad, tattle tail!" the professor jabbed.

"Oh ya, we'll see about that," I replied, and I sat down in a chair next to his desk and watched out the window overlooking the parking lot.

It couldn't have been more than 2 minutes when I noticed Verdi briskly walking toward the Science building.

"Oh boy, now you're in trouble!" I chuckled.

I could hear the echo of Verdi's stiletto high heel shoes marching up the stairs, and heading our way down the empty hallway and then into the professor's office.

"I jus get a call to take care of sum ting," she simply stated, and she focused in on the professor.

"Go back to Cuba, and pick some bananas you commie whore dog," the professor jeered as he leaned back in his chair and put his foot on his desk.

She instantly grabbed his foot, and flipped him over in his chair. He did a sort of backward somersault onto the floor! Before he could get up, Verdi pounced on him, and literally began beating him to death with the telephone she had taken off his desk! He struggled aimlessly to fight her off, but she was just too vicious!

"Don't kill him before I get the mineral sample I need!" I shouted.

Professor Prygocci was literally a massive hematoma and Verdi wasn't done with him yet!

She dragged his limp body by his neck tie back to his flipped over chair, and she pulled him onto it upside down so his back was against the seat and his legs were over the backrest. She then lifted the chair back up onto its squeaky wheels! The professor was awkwardly upside down in the chair with his legs folded over the back of the chair, and his back was on the seat with his head hanging down toward the floor!

She pulled him out of his office by his neck tie as he was upside down in his rolling chair! She began wheeling him through the halls of the science building, and followed me over to the radiation laboratory, until we finally stopped in front of the radioactive material vault!

"Go open it!" she shouted at the semi conscious professor.

"Screw you, Bitch!" he moaned.

That obviously didn't sit well with Verdi. As she was still holding his necktie in her hand, she vigorously began swinging him around in a circle as he was still trapped in his roller chair! With each revolution, his velocity was massively increasing! Faster and faster he went around! Finally she let him go, and he went crashing into the vault door, busting him and the chair into pieces!

Bewildered, the professor struggled to his feet, and clumsily turned the dial to the proper combination on the vaults lock. The lever that kept the door closed made a clunk like sound. It was now open.

"Now ju get out a here, Perroggi!" she shouted.

The professor staggered aimlessly out of the room, desperately trying to hold himself together.

"I tol ju someday I gonna kick his ass!" stated Verdi as she left the room. I put on a heavy lead lined radiation suit and I entered the vault. It was filled with dozens of lead pig containers with bright orange Radiation warning labels attached.

I quickly glanced through them until I found the container labeled "Uraninite". Then I closed the vault, and placed the mineral in a spectrometer.

After a lot of tweaking I was able to isolate a small fragment of Francium. I placed the sample into the particle accelerator that was in the room, and after about 14 hours I had a small sample of an element. I placed it into the spectrometer and it was 99.9% pure Astatine!

I needed to work fast so I placed the specimen in a lead container and rushed back to my lab. The main problem was there was so little of it, I didn't know if it was going to be enough.

I began mixing the antiserum, and injected a micro grain into a Silver Orchid test rabbit.

Miraculously, it seemed to rejuvenate its cells and it did become somewhat younger again. I'm just not sure how much its body rejuvenated, but it definitely went in the right direction. I don't have enough to spare for another test, but I'm confident I have this right.

Chapter 49

It was 3 AM and pitch dark out when I called and woke up Crystal. I told her to go get Kelly, and meet me at the old cement factory in 2 hours.

"I have an antiserum but it's going to degrade in 3 hours so please don't be late. This is the only chance we will have, and I only have enough for one try," I urgently stated.

"Okay, we'll be there! Thank you so much, Donny!" she replied.

"Please don't bring anyone else. Just you and Kelly, okay," I stated.

"Do you think it will work, Donny?" she hopefully questioned.

"No, I don't think it will work…I know it will work! I'm just not sure how far back to normal I can bring you girls. Just be there on time, please!" and I hung up the phone.

I quickly gathered my things, and placed a few syringes into my doctor's bag along with the radioactive antiserum which was stored in a glass vial and enclosed in a lead pig container.

As I headed for the door, I heard a tired voice coming from Verdi's room.

"Where do ju tink ju are goin?" she sleepily stated.

"I have to go to the science lab, but I should be right back," I nervously replied.

"Okay kid, just make sure ju come right back," she said, as she fell back to sleep.

"Holy crap! That was really easy!" I thought as I headed to the secret garage.

When I arrived there I rushed to put the key into the automatic gate opener but for some reason the gate would not open!

"This is just great! I need to get my car out and Verdi switched keys on me!" I said to myself.

I noticed a pack of matches lying on the ground, and I instinctively began breaking off the match heads and packed them in, one by one into the keyhole of the gate opener. I saved the last match and stood to the side of the lock and I prayed as I lit the last match.

I stretched my arm out and touched it to the keyhole!

There was a quick snap-like explosion, unlike the loud "Kabooms" that I am now used to, but it was enough to break the lock open.

I quickly found the trigger wires and twisted them together. The gate immediately began to rise!

With no time to lose, I raced into my car and took off!

There was no traffic and I managed to make it to the cement factory in a little under 2 hours, but there was no one there yet.

I was nervous sitting there in the dark, but after about 10 minutes I could see that the sun was about to rise. The darkness was beginning to dissipate a bit. I could hear the birds begin to chirp, and the dawn morning was about to arrive.

That's when I noticed a small beat up car quickly driving into the cement factory parking lot. There were two silhouettes in the front seat, and as it got closer, I could see it was Kelly and Crystal.

I nervously got out of my car, and Crystal jumped out of the passenger seat, and ran over to embrace me. Kelly just sat in her car, and appeared apprehensive about getting out.

"Don't freakin' look at me Donny! I don't want you to see me like this," Kelly stated. I walked around the car, and opened her door.

"Come out Kelly. It's all going to be okay," I softly spoke.

The sun was rising, and I could see her old withered face, and the red wash in her eyes.

"Look what has become of me Donny. I guess maybe I should have changed my ways and become a "good girl" like you wanted," she sarcastically stated.

"It wasn't your fault Kelly. It was my fault. If I would have had the guts to knock on your door after that day at the waterfall, everything would have been different, and I'm the one to blame!

But now, I'm here to give you a fresh start. Hopefully, I'll get you your years back, and I'll help you get off the drugs, but you need to help me too. You have to want to clean yourself up," I stated.

"I will Donny. I promise you I will make a fresh start!" she exclaimed.

Just then, I oddly heard the trunk of Kelly's car unlatch, and it opened by itself!

Out rolled an elderly man who was hiding in the trunk, and holding a sawed off shotgun.

He pointed it at me as he limped around to the front of the car.

"Kenny is that you?" I curiously asked.

"I didn't know Kenny was in there, Donny! When I called Kelly she insisted on picking me up. Now I understand why!" Crystal exclaimed.

"Sorry Crystal, but Kenny and I need this antiserum more than you!" Kelly harshly stated and she pushed her towards me.

"Crystal, you move over next to Donny,... now!" Kenny demanded.

Kenny limped over to Kelly, and told her to go into my car, and get the antiserum as he kept his gun trained on us.

"Geez Kenny, sorry you still have the gimpy limp that Marco laid on you," I jeered.

"Shut up school boy! I should have knocked you off back in high school," he replied.

Kelly quickly found my medical bag with the antiserum and returned with it next to Kenny's side.

"Sorry about this Crystal, I know you were trying to be a good friend, but you have your blue blood family to take care of you, and I unfortunately, only have Kenny," Kelly stated.

"Okay Lord, how does this stuff work?" Kenny demanded. He opened up the doctor's bag, and removed the two syringes and the lead container containing the antiserum.

"I'm not going to tell you, so you can forget about it," I shouted.

Kenny then pointed his shotgun at Crystal's head.

"Have it your way Lord, I got nothin' to lose at this point," and he began to pull back the trigger!

"Okay, okay! Put the gun down, and I'll tell you!" I shouted, and Kenny pointed the gun back at my face.

"Start singin' Lord," ordered Kenny.

"One cc per ten year reduction. The drug is very strong. But, I only have enough to do the girls, which was 4cc's for Kelly and 2cc's for Crystal. There isn't enough for you Kenny," I stated.

"So 6 cc's would bring me back 60 years?" questioned Kenny.

If someone used up the whole 6 cc's, yes," I replied.

Kenny turned to Kelly, and pointed his gun at her.

"Get over there with them Kelly," Kenny ordered.

"Are you shitting me! You bastard!! You're going to cut me out, after I'm the one who let you in on this?!!" she scolded.

"Sorry Babe, I figure you had a lot to do with me getting busted all those times for your drugs. I'm looking out for my ass for a change, so move it!" Kenny shouted.

"Yeah your ass is on the back of your hand, butt-r-fingers!" Kelly replied.

The three of us stood there trembling as dawn broke. Kenny was becoming frustrated as he was fiddling around with a syringe and trying to open the lead radiation container, as he held his gun on us. Finally he gave up, and tossed it back into my doctor's bag.

"Get over here and shoot me up Lord," Kenny demanded.

He kept the gun trained on Crystal, as he handed me the bag.

"What's going to happen after I inject you Kenny?" I nervously asked.

"I'm going to let you guys go," he sarcastically stated.

I had no choice, so I carefully removed the vial of antiserum from the lead container.

The color of the antiserum was still fine, but I knew that there wasn't much time left before the half life of the AT85 was going to begin to expire. I filled a syringe as Kenny was pulling up his sleeve.

"Okay, do it Lord!" he ordered.

I brought the syringe closer toward his wrinkly needle tracked arm and prepared to inject him.

"Stop!!" he shouted.

I instantly stopped, and thought that maybe his conscience got the better of him.

"If I have a bad reaction from this shit, it would give you an opportunity to take my gun and turn it on me! I'll need to kill the three of you first, and then I'll inject myself," Kenny smugly stated.

Then, he quickly snatched the syringe out of my hand.

"Get back over there, with your girlfriends!" Kenny snickered.

The three of us stood there terrified as Kenny was aiming his shot gun at us.

"Now turn around! I don't want to see your pretty faces when I blow your heads off!" he chuckled.

"Donny, I'm so sorry!" Crystal cried.

"Kenny! Stop it right now! How could you do this to me after all we've been through?" Kelly demanded.

"Any last words Lord, before I kill you losers?" Kenny jeered.

"Yes Kenny, I just noticed that "El Verdugo" is coming up right behind you, and I think you should put the gun down, or you will be dead in 5 seconds," I calmly stated.

"Nice try, Lord, but what the hell is an "El Verdugo? Your fairy godmother?" Kenny chuckled.

"It's a Spanish word. It means "The Assassin," I replied.

Kenny's face became puzzled, and he began to look over his shoulder to see if there was actually someone behind him. Verdi pulled her trigger, and put a bullet into the back of his head, blowing apart his brain and medulla oblongata. His knees seemed to crumble beneath him as he instantly dropped dead to the ground!

I quickly grabbed the syringe out of Kenny's hand, and quickly injected Crystal and then Kelly.

In a matter of seconds they both fell to the ground, and the transformation was beginning.

Crystal first showed signs of rejuvenating as her skin and muscle tone began to return. Kelly was also showing signs of regression, and after about 10 minutes the transformation was nearly complete.

The red wash in their eyes also diminished, but in Kelly's case there was still just a hint of it.

"Don't ju do dat to me again, Donny! Ju could get me in big trouble!" Verdi exclaimed.

"I'm sorry, I promise to be good from now on! How did you find me?" I exclaimed as I rushed over to hug her.

"What ju talkin' about, mang? I'm da CIA. If I can't find you, nobody can. Besides dey put a tracking device in jur car before dey give it to ju," she coolly stated.

As we were preparing to leave, an army of black sedans swarmed into the cement factory, and several large men wearing black suits and sunglasses jumped out of their cars.

Two of the men picked up, and threw Kenny's body into the trunk of a car. While the others checked out the girls vital signs, and made sure everyone was okay.

"Mr. None Of Ju Business ain't going to like dis," Verdi regretfully stated.

"Really? I just possibly created the Fountain of Youth, and it belongs to the United States government. I think he'll be okay with it," I replied.

"Dats not what I mean, Donny. Dees girls were given da Silver Orchid for a reason. Ju are messing wid da system. Dey will probably send dem right to prison," she stated.

"I'll work this out later with the Senator. For now can you bring them back to our place so I can keep an eye on them for any side effects that might occur," I stated, and she reluctantly nodded her head, and said "yes".

I then turned my attention back to the girls.

"Go with Verdi now, before the cops show up!" I shouted.

The girls scrambled, and quickly followed Verdi to her hidden car and they quickly left.

A dark Limo arrived, and the Senator got out.

"What's going on here, Donny?" sternly stated the Senator.

"Well, I have good news and bad news for you Senator.

I was able to create an antiserum for the DLSO," I stated.

"And which part of the good or bad news is that?" he angrily questioned.

"Well, the good news is, if someone is mistakenly convicted, their years can be given back to them. And, if I can continue my research,

I just might be able to figure out a way to revert the onset of aging, and possibly certain age related diseases," I confidently stated.

"Hmm, my father has Alzheimer's disease. Do you think it might work on that?" the Senator questioned.

"I'll try my best, but how does the Fountain of Youth sound to you, Senator," I replied.

"Okay, okay! So then what's the bad news?" the Senator reluctantly asked.

"I don't have any more element At85, and it's ores are really scarce. I'll need more to continue my research, especially if I am working on a cure for Alzheimer's disease, Senator," I stated.

"Okay Donny, anything else?" inquired the Senator.

"Yes, just one more thing...Those two girls, Kelly Mosley and Crystal Mckune. I would appreciate it if their records were wiped clean, and given a fresh start. I feel a little responsible for their predicament," I stated.

The Senator looked down at the ground and thought for a moment.

"Okay Genius, consider it done. Now get back to your lab and I'll talk to some people about getting you more of that At85, whatever that is," the Senator chuckled.

I hugged the Senator, and then I immediately hopped in my Corvette and left the cement factory.

Chapter 50

I drove as fast as I could, hoping to catch up to Verdi, but when I finally arrived at our apartment, they were nowhere to be found. About an hour passed, when I could hear Verdi coming up the stairs, talking to someone. When the door opened, only Verdi and Crystal were standing there, and I was star struck by Crystal's awesome beauty.

"Crystal you, you look amazing!" I stuttered.

"Remember how geeky I was in high school? Thank you Donny, for bringing me back to my true age. I never dreamt I'd have a second chance," she emotionally stated and she began to cry.

I noticed Verdi was carrying a grocery bag, but someone was missing!

"Where's Kelly!" I exclaimed.

"We stopped for groceries, and she took off out the back door of the store! We looked for her for over an hour, but she was gone," declared Crystal shrugging her shoulders and shaking her head in disbelief.

"Where do you think she went?" I fearfully asked.

"Probably back to her dump crack house friends, I suppose," Crystal replied.

I couldn't believe that Kelly had run off and disappeared. I'm concerned that something might happen to her, since the antiserum was still somewhat unstable.

"That stupid girl can never do the right thing! She promised me she was going to clean up her act," I dismally stated.

Verdi then went into the kitchen and made us some sandwiches for lunch.

Afterward, Crystal and I sat down on the couch in our living room. We talked for some time and Crystal became tired and she laid down on the couch and rested her beautiful head on my lap and she fell asleep.

She was so beautiful and she smelled so good. It reminded me of the strawberry perfume the girls at Chess King were wearing.

As she slept, I just sat there and caressed her beautiful auburn hair. After about an hour or so the phone rang and Verdi took the call. She spoke quietly and briefly, and then quickly hung up.

"Who was that?" I whispered.

"None Of Jur Business," she stated.

"Since when is it not my business!" I harshly whispered, as not to wake up Crystal.

"No you idiote'! Dat was 'none Of Jur Business!' he asked what happened about de girls. If dey okay, and if…de antiserum worked permanente," she stated.

Just then Crystal's eyes slowly began to open, and she smiled as she held my hand. I don't know what came over me, but as I gazed into her light green eyes, and I moved a few strands of her hair away from her face, I became hypnotized by her beauty. I moved to lay next to her and I kissed her. She wrapped her arms around me, and held me tightly. I could feel the warmth of her body pressing against mine, and after all that we had been through, I never imagined Crystal would ever be lying next to me and in my arms.

"Hey Donny, can we finally go out tonight, and get that pizza, I won?" she sarcastically whispered.

"That depends, what kind of pizza do you like?" I replied.

"Definitely Pepperoni!" she laughed.

From that day on, Crystal and I were inseparable, and so our romance began.

I continued working on my projects, and Crystal had enrolled at a nearby college.

A few months had passed since that morning when Kelly ran off, and I often wondered whatever became of her. I still sometimes think about her. Even though I am totally in love with Crystal, I could never forget that summer day with Kelly at my secret waterfall.

Chapter 51

The phone abruptly rang just as I was measuring a radical chemical element to deposit into a boiling beaker of acid.

"Damm this always happens when I'm doing something intricate!" I thought.

When I answered the phone, I was surprised to hear Marco's voice.

"Yo Donny!" he shouted.

"Marco, what's up dude?" I laughed.

"Hey listen, out of nowhere I found a letter stuck in my mailbox. It was from Kelly Mosely," he stated.

"Did you read it? What does it say? Where is she? Is she okay?" I erratically inquired.

"On the envelope it just says... 'Marco please give this letter to Donny as soon as possible...Kelly'".

"Well open it, and read it to me, man!" I exclaimed.

I could hear Marco tearing the envelope apart and unfolding the paper.

"Okay this is what it says," Marco read on.

"Dear Donny,

I'm so sorry I ran off from your Bodyguard and Crystal at the store. I don't know why I did, but it probably has something to do with me never being able to make the right choices in my life. I saw how you looked at Crystal, and I realized that you and her were meant to be together. Not us. I've been such a terrible person to my family, my friends, myself, and the one person who really cared the most about me, you. I'm so sorry for the way that I treated you in high school. I wish I could say that it wasn't really me, but I had so much anger toward you, because I thought you didn't love me the same way I loved you, and you didn't want to be with me. I wish I had a time machine, and could turn back time, and go back to that summer when we were kids. Just you and me, together forever at your secret waterfall.

Donny, that was the best day of my life and I was with you. Later, when I saw you drive your bike past my house those following weeks, I wished I had the courage to run outside and tell you how I felt about you. Instead I blamed you for everything! It was your fault you didn't like me! It was your fault I was with Kenny! It was your fault I was on drugs! And it was your fault that I'm a mess! I blamed you for everything bad in my life. But I was wrong. I feel empty now and alone. I have no real friends or family that want anything to do with me. I just wanted to tell you that I really appreciate everything you have done for me. I'm sorry I couldn't keep my promise and stop using drugs. I tried kicking the stuff, but for some reason it's the only thing that makes me feel good about myself. Maybe in another life we can be together Donny, but until then, I just want you to know...I love you so much Donny Lord, and I always will. XOXO...Kelly."

"That's it," said Marco.

"Where is she Marco!" I shouted.

"How the hell am I supposed to know!" he shouted back.

"That sounds to me like a suicide letter! You need to call the police!" I exclaimed.

"Okay, I'll call the cops. It's against my nature but I'll do it for you," he replied.

I heard the door of our apartment open, and Crystal had just come home from school. She saw that I was upset and asked me what was wrong.

"I think Kelly left a suicide note for me today in Marco's mailbox! He just read it to me, and I told him to call the police! Come on let's go! We have to try to find her!" I exclaimed.

We quickly left and I drove as fast as I could back to Bakersfield.

"Where do you think she could be?" I questioned Crystal.

"She might be held up in one of the crack houses she frequents," replied Crystal.

Just before we hit Bakersfield I stopped at a gas station, and called Marco from a pay phone.

"Marco did you call the police?!" I exclaimed.

"I did, but the lazy cop said, unless she has been missin' for 24 hours, there was nothin' they would do," replied Marco.

"We're on our way back to Bakersfield to look for her. Can you check with your sources to see if anyone has seen Kelly around?" I asked.

"Will do, Donny. Say "Hi" to Crystal for me," and he hung up the phone.

After about two hours of driving, we finally made it to Bakersfield, and we began searching for Kelly.

Crystal informed me that there was an area known to be a druggie hang out at the pavilion in a nearby park; Recreation Park. The addicts referred to it as, "Wreck Park". I supposed that title fit, since their lives were a wreck.

When we drove over to the pavilion, there was a group of degenerates sitting on the picnic tables under the pavilion, listening to loud heavy metal music, smoking pot and drinking beer. I struggled to see if Kelly was in there with them.

"Come on, let's go ask them if they have seen Kelly!" I exclaimed.

We left the car and approached the group. It was a mix of teenagers and young adults, thirteen to twenty something years old, a combination of degenerate boys and girls. As we approached, they instantly became suspicious and started hiding their drug paraphernalia and liquor.

"Hey a couple of Narc's just showed up!" someone shouted.

"Have any of you seen Kelly Mosely?" I called out.

"Get lost pigs!" a voice shouted from the crowd. Then a few others joined in with some other creative derogatory remarks.

"Listen! Kelly is in trouble, and we need to find her!" I pleaded.

"We don't know any Kelly-Mo-belly" a girl shouted, and the crowd began laughing.

"Come on this is useless. She's not here, lets go," I stated.

We left the park and Crystal had an idea.

"Maybe she went home to her parents?" declared Crystal.

"Let's go see, it's worth a try, and I turned the car around and we headed toward my old street.

I drove slowly hoping to maybe catch a glimpse of her walking or sitting by the roadside. I mentioned to Crystal that we would have to stop off at my parent's house, since we were driving right past it. But first we had to check Kelly's house.

I turned onto our street, and quickly accelerated toward Kelly's parents' home. When I pulled into their driveway, I could see her mother peeking out from behind the window curtain, wondering who had just pulled into their driveway driving a Corvette.

It was awkward walking up the steps to Kelly's house. Even though I had done this hundreds of times when we were kids. This time it felt as if something was terribly wrong.

Crystal rang the doorbell, and both of Kelly's parents answered the door. When the door opened the strong odor of cigarette fumes overwhelmed me, and I remembered that they were both heavy chain smokers.

"Hi Mr. and Mrs. Mosely, I don't know if you remember me. I'm Donny Lord from down the Street, and I think you know Crystal," I stated.

"Yes Donny, of course we remember you. We heard that you are doing very well at Caltech," Mrs. Mosely noted.

"Yes, thank you. Uhm, is Kelly here? We are looking for her, and it's really urgent that we find her," I strongly stated.

"Sorry, we haven't seen nor heard from Kelly in a few years. She stole some of my wife's jewelry and other valuable things to support her drug habit. We had no choice but to kick her out," sighed Mr. Mosely.

"Well, Kelly left a disturbing note with a friend of mine, and we are afraid she might try to hurt herself!" I reported.

"Oh no! Do you have any idea where else she could be?!" Mrs. Mosely frantically asked.

"As far as I'm concerned, she made her bed, and she can sleep in it. She's probably held up somewhere with some drug junkies, and she's just probably trying to hustle you out of some cash," Mr. Mosely harshly stated.

"No, I don't think so, but we will keep on looking for her," I said.

"If we find her, we'll let you know that she's safe," said Crystal.

Her parents were puffing away at their cigarettes as they quickly closed the door behind them.

"No wonder why Kelly turned out the way she did. She probably could never find her parents through all that cigarette smoke," I stated.

Crystal shook her head, and raised her eyebrows in agreement.

"Come on, let's stop by and see my parents. Maybe my mom might have an idea where to find her," I said.

I drove down the street and saw Mr. Bundy, he was old and hunched over like a zombie as he walked a tiny Chihuahua down the sidewalk. It was pretty clear that he had been injected with the DLSO. I wondered who else in the neighborhood might have gotten it too. Probably most of the North end gang, I presumed.

I turned into my parent's driveway and shut off the car. My parents came running out of the house, surprised and excited to see us.

"What are you kids doing here! Come on inside you two!" fawned my mother.

We all sat down at the kitchen table, and I told my parents that Kelly was missing. Just then I noticed my father was wearing the dilapidated "Ass, Gas or Grass tee shirt," I had given to him years ago before I left for college.

"I thought you lost that shirt Dad?" I chuckled.

"Can you imagine that somehow it was hiding behind the washing machine," he sarcastically stated, and he gave my mother a nasty look.

"So where do you think Kelly could be?" inquired my mother.

"I don't know, but she left a letter for me with Marco. She seemed depressed and suicidal, which worries me," I stated.

"Was there anything else?" questioned my father.

I sat back in the chair, and thought intensely about the words that Marco had recited to me.

"She talked about being at my secret waterfall in the woods when we were kids," I simply stated.

"Oh my god! She said that was the best day of her life! Dad, call the police!"

I jumped up and ran out the back door into the woods. The sun was just beginning to set, and its final rays of the day beamed down through the branches of the forest. I could hear Crystal's footsteps running right behind me, as I crashed through the overgrown vegetation that had now engulfed my path which led to the waterfall. As I approached the final rise which concealed my secret waterfall, I could finally hear the sound of water rushing over the fall and crashing into the pond below. It was a tranquil sound, and it brought me back to that summer day with Kelly.

When I finally reached the top of the slope, the sun was almost gone.

I could vaguely see the silhouette of a slender woman, hanging by her neck from a rope attached to a tree limb, just off the edge of the waterfall.

Crystal began screaming and crying! "KELLY! KELLY!" at the top of her lungs. I just dropped to my knees and my eyes began filling with tears.

I looked down, and noticed that I was at the exact location where Kelly and I had climbed out of the pond soaking wet that special day. I laid myself down on that spot, and stared into the dark sky, hoping to see a sign that Kelly was now free.

Crystal came over, and laid down beside me, and we held each other and cried.

A few minutes later I could hear my father and the police shouting in the woods, while looking for us.

"Over here! Come quickly!" Crystal jumped up, and shouted.

I just continued laying there in the soft grass crying as I stared into the heavens, as they cut Kelly down from the tree limb.

I didn't want to see her that way. I just wanted to remember her from the time of "The best day of our lives". When we were together here at the waterfall, laughing and holding hands ever so tightly, as we laid on this soft blanket of grass and watched the clouds as they floated past us. Crystal sat next to me and continued to cry. I sat up and put my arm around her. I told her that there was nothing anyone could have done for Kelly. The moment Kenny asked her out, and she chose to be with him, her fate was sealed.

Chapter 52

Several days had passed and we all gathered back in Bakersfield to attend Kelly's funeral.

It wasn't extraordinary, in fact, it was quite small, and only a few people attended. Besides her parents, my parents, Crystal and I, there were a few of the usual show ups. Aunts, uncles, and a few cousins. But none of her so-called "friends" were there.

The drug addicts and lowlifes she felt a close kinship with were finally gone from her life, and now she was surrounded by those who truly did love and care about her.

Her casket was open, and wild flowers surrounded her as she silently laid in peace. Crystal stayed close to me, but then let me go by myself when it was time to say goodbye to Kelly.

I waited for my turn as her family members said their goodbyes and prayed for her.

When it was my turn, I slowly approached her. It took all my might to hold back my tears and have the strength to keep from breaking down.

I stood next to her lifeless body and leaned over her and took her cold hand in mine, and held it as tightly as she had once held mine.

I whispered in her ear of a wonderful dream that I had, and I told her that I was keeping it in my heart, and it was only for her to hear.

"I told her it was the first day of high school, and I got on the school bus. We hadn't seen each other in three years, since that glorious day at the waterfall. You were anxiously waiting for me, and when our eyes met you smiled and asked me to sit with you. There was so much energy between us, we couldn't take our eyes off each other, and you took my hand and held it tightly. I told you that I've been waiting a long time for this moment, and I leaned over and kissed you.

"I love you so much, Kelly," I gushed.

"I love you so much too, Donny Lord!" she replied.

Suddenly I realized that the bus had stopped and it was totally empty now. You were instantly wearing a beautiful white jeweled wedding dress adorned with wild flowers, and I was wearing a long tailed white tuxedo.

The bus doors opened, and we walked down the aisle together and down the steps of the bus, stepping outside next to our secret waterfall.

The sun was shining brightly and I could hear the birds singing, and the wind was gently blowing your hair away from you. The jewels that adorned your dress were sparkling brilliantly and you looked so beautiful.

There was a group of faceless people all dressed in white suits and white dresses. They surrounded an Altar made up of white and lavender roses and light blue ribbons.

Everyone turned as we approached them, and began clapping their hands. Our parents were there and a minister too. We walked hand in hand towards them and the crowd opened as we walked to the Altar. As we stood under the canopy, I held both of your hands and we stared into each other's eyes and you smiled. I knew then I was forever with my soul mate and the love of my life. Now we would finally be together, forever my love,"

I paused for a moment to wipe away my tears...

"Sadly, it was just a dream Kelly, but how I wish I would have had the courage to knock on your door, on any one of the days that followed our time at the waterfall, and taken you in my arms, and told you that I was in love with you," I mournfully confessed.

I whispered a few more loving words to her. Words that were special secrets, and only between Kelly and me. Then I leaned over and caressed her soft hair and kissed her on her cheek. I suddenly realized that that kiss was the first and only time I had ever kissed her. I began to tear up and cry, when I felt a warm hand take mine, and when I looked over, Crystal was there beside me.

I try to understand why things happen the way they do. It's frustrating to me, and trust me, I'm a genius, and even I can't figure out what's going on in this unpredictable life we live. Some say everything happens for a reason. But I can't find any good reason for people we love to die.

I took Crystal to the side and I held her hands, and I spoke to her.

"Crystal, even though I had that moment with Kelly at the waterfall, I realized that it was just a moment, and wasn't meant to be. I'll always cherish that moment with Kelly, and she will always hold a very special place in me.

But my heart belongs to you, Crystal".

We hugged as Mrs. Mosely approached us. She was reaching into her purse, and she handed me a folded up piece of paper.

"I think Kelly would like you to have this Donny," she sadly stated and she handed me the paper, and walked away.

When I opened it, I saw that it was a colored pencil drawing done by a young girl.

It was of a sunny sky scattered with fluffy white clouds floating by, birds flying overhead and a pond with a beautiful waterfall. And us, lying together on the grassy shore, holding hands, and staring up into the sky, watching the clouds and smiling. There were small pink hearts floating around our heads and we appeared to be so happy and in love.

Underneath she wrote...

"I Love You Donny Lord!!! Together forever!!! XOXOX!!!!".

I was overwhelmed, and I got all choked up. I told Crystal that I needed to step outside for some fresh air and I wanted to be alone.

She understood and let me go off by myself.

I walked out of the funeral home's door, and found myself on the sidewalk next to the main street.

Cars were quickly driving past me, and I couldn't help but to think about how their lives were just going on as usual, without any sadness or worries in the world.

Poor Kelly is laying inside this funeral home, dead in a box, and I am so devastated.

I turned to return to the funeral home, when I heard a city commuter bus's brakes squeal and stop behind me at the curb.

Out of the corner of my eye, I noticed there was a "BUS STOP" sign on the curb behind me, and the bus driver had stopped to pick me up.

"Ya getting on or what shit for brains?" the bus driver rudely called out.

When I turned back to tell the bus driver I wasn't getting on, I quickly noticed a much older but familiar face. It was Dwain, my old school bus driver!

I was taken aback since he was so much older looking, and obviously a DLSO recipient.

"Well if it isn't Dwain the insane! Still stuck driving a bus I see!" I jeered.

"Holy shit on fire! If it isn't Donny "Dip Shit" Lord," Dwain exclaimed.

"I see you took the DLSO hit Dwain, and I have a secret to tell you! I invented that monster juice they stuck into your vein!" I sarcastically chuckled.

"Oh that's sweet! Thanks man, you kept me out of the joint. I would have been stuck there for the next 30 years! Come on up let me shake your hand, no hard feelings!" exclaimed Dwain.

"Sure, no hard feelings," I said as I quickly jumped up to get on the bus, and shake his outstretched hand! Suddenly the door slammed shut, and I crashed right into the tempered glass and steel door. Dwain quickly reopened the door and brutally pushed me back from the bus, and I fell flat onto the ground!

As blood poured from my nose, I watched the bus quickly accelerate past me, and I heard Dwain hysterically laughing out loud and he shouted "What a Bozo!" as he hastily drove off.

I just rolled over and sat there on the curb, wiping the blood gushing from my nose, when I noticed the bus was once again stopping, about a half a block down the street.

A mysterious woman was patiently waiting at the next bus stop. She was wearing a white cotton sundress with a floral scarf over her head, large black Ray Ban sunglasses, and she was smoking a big fat Cuban cigar. I saw the bus door open, and before she got on, she aggressively threw her lit cigar at Dwain as she was stepping up onto the bus! Then I heard the tumult begin! Dwain was viciously getting the shit kicked out of him! The bus was rocking from side to side as Dwain was flung around the interior of the bus and being beaten to a pulp!

I just smiled and whispered, "Ju go girl, Ju go!!"

"Definitely Pepperoni."

Note from the Author

Although this was a fictional story, it was inspired by a beautiful, kind hearted teenage girl that lived in my neighborhood in the late 1970's.

She had everything going for her until she fell in with the wrong crowd, and she was exposed to drugs.
As the years progressed, she became more of an addict, and continued on the unfortunate path that she chose which ultimately consumed her.
Sadly, several years ago I was informed that she couldn't handle her drug addicted life anymore and she committed suicide.
I was really heart broken when I heard the news.
Such a shame, such a waste of a life.

Books by B.L. Blocher:

The Watchmaker

Coming Soon:

The Watchmaker part 2 (The Chosen)
As The Sparrows Fly
Razzle Dazzle